Prem Kutowaroo was born and educated in
Mauritius. In 19⁵ᵗ ... ... a student nurse in
the so... of ... with patients with
learn... ...ears he left nursing
... ...ed in the accounts
...panies in London. He then
... ...nd now works part-time for
... ...nd also in security. Among his
... ...chievements are a BA (Hons) in
... ...nces from Middlesex Polytechnic (now
... ...ity) and the Open University, an MSc in
...rprofessional Health and Welfare Studies (South
... ...k University) and an MPhil (Brunel University).
... ...e lives in Bracknell, Berkshire.

By the same author:

Pangs of Life, The Book Guild, 2003

IN SEARCH OF LOVE

Prem Kutowaroo

The Book Guild Ltd
Sussex, England

First published in Great Britain in 2005 by
The Book Guild Ltd
25 High Street
Lewes, East Sussex
BN7 2LU

Typesetting in Baskerville by
Keyboard Services, Luton, Bedfordshire

Printed in Great Britain by
Athenaeum Press Ltd, Gateshead

A catalogue record for this book is available from
The British Library

ISBN 1 85776 920 1

CONTENTS

1

City Life and my New Neighbours

I lived at the flat for ten years. It was in the western part of the capital city of Port-Louis in Mauritius, a place called Cassis with a neighbouring beach called La Saline. I lived in a two-bedroomed house with a separate kitchen, bathroom, and an outside pit toilet. The house was in a quiet lane away from the main road, giving me the feeling of living in the countryside. My neighbours were nice and friendly and didn't care what I did for a living. I always felt safe amongst them, even though they knew that I was doing an immoral job.

My life started to change when one of my neighbours, an elderly man, moved away to live with his son as he was getting too old to look after himself. I missed him, because he was such a nice person to talk to. I used to help him clean his house and do some gardening and also go shopping for him. He was like a father to me and he always used to say, 'Daughter, I hope you'll find true happiness one day. Keep faith in God.'

The new neighbours who moved in were a couple in their early fifties and their son. I guess the son to be in his thirties – about my age – and single. They were friendly and came to introduce themselves to me when they first came to live there. When they found out that I lived on my own, they invited me round for tea. After the first visit to their place, I made it a habit to visit them quite often, hoping to met Jeet, their son. But every time I went there, he was at work. Something in him attracted me and I couldn't tell what it was. I thought it was because he was of medium build and had blue eyes, a feature that was not so common among people of Indian origin, and, most probably, because he had a mature way of talking to people. I didn't think too much about it, but when I looked into his eyes, something stirred in me. I had met quite a few men, but I hadn't felt like this before. I realised he had also become interested in me, when one day there was a knock at the door and it was him.

'Good morning. Are you free?' he asked.

'Good morning. Yes, I'm free. Why?' I replied.

'As I wasn't doing anything I thought I would like to talk to you, Rakhi.'

This worried me a bit because I didn't know whether he was making a social call or had come to make use of my job – I didn't usually associate my job with neighbours – or wanted to talk to me about myself. For some reason, I thought that he was going to complain about something.

'Yes, sure, Jeet,' I replied. 'Come in. What's the matter?'

'Thanks. Nothing really. I just wanted to talk to you.'

'Come and sit down. Tell me what you were going to tell me,' I said calmly, sitting opposite him.

'I don't know how to tell you this, but I seem to have developed strong feelings towards you ever since I set eyes on you, Rakhi.'

2

My heart thumped and the energy drew me to my feet. I went quiet for few seconds, and I nearly choked in surprise and disbelief. I felt emotional because no one had approached me in that way since I had moved to Port-Louis.

I also gave a sigh of relief because he had not come to complain about anything, and certainly not to make use of my job. He seemed a nice person to talk to.

'Are you all right, Rakhi?' Jeet asked.

'Yes,' I replied with a slight tremble in my voice. 'It's just that no one has spoken to me like that before.'

'Sorry, Rakhi. I didn't mean to upset you, but I thought I would talk to you about it as you're an approachable person.'

'Is that all you wanted to say, Jeet?'

'No, Rakhi. I know that you might be surprised but I would like to know all about you. I would like to know, if you don't mind, how you managed to get into this sort of job. You appear to be a respectable person and not cut out for it.'

I was surprised that a person I was speaking to for the first time wanted to know the story of my life. I was impressed by his approach and we started talking as if we'd known each other for some time.

'You mean, prostitution?' I asked.

'If you put it that way!' he replied. 'Something tells me that you're in the wrong job.'

'Are you sure you want to know about me?'

'Yes, Rakhi. So long as you are honest and truthful about it.'

'Jeet, you sound a nice person. I can talk to you. No one has bothered to find out why I started this way of life. I've felt just like a toy doll in a corner.

3

Everyone uses it when they want to, but no one has bothered to find out what it's worth.'

'You may be right, Rakhi.'

'Since you're willing to hear my story,' I continued, 'I'll tell you all about it. I must tell you, though, that I've found most men appear nice until they get what they want. Then they don't want to know you. It's not that I wanted something from them, but that's what I think they're like.'

'Thanks, Rakhi, but you can't always say that,' Jeet replied.

'I can say that from experience, Jeet. It's a long story. I'll tell you when I've got more time. What I want to know from you, if you want to tell me, is why you are still single.'

I surprised myself, asking about him during this first meeting. He didn't seem to mind. He started telling me about himself.

'I don't have a long story, but it's just that I haven't met the right person to be my *rani* [queen] yet. My parents have talked to me several times about getting married, but they always get the same answer – I haven't met the right person yet. You know the custom in Mauritius that people get married to someone they don't know. There is no love marriage and they grow to love each other after they are married. If things don't work out, they still have to put on a brave face and live with it for the sake of the parents and respect.'

'I know,' I replied. 'It's a common practice. It's a way of life. You can't change it.'

'I know,' Jeet continued. 'People call it arranged marriage. You choose girls as you choose a dress in a market, but girls do not get the chance to choose boys. I've promised that I won't get married to

4

someone I don't know. You know what they say to me?'

'What?' I asked.

'They say that if I think like that I'll never get married and I'll grow old without having any children for myself. "I know", I say to them. "It's better to die like that than to face the ordeal of getting married to someone you don't know and probably may not like."'

'You know what, Jeet?' I said.

'What?' he inquired.

'If you think like that you'll never get married,' I joked.

'Oh shut up!' he laughed.

I gradually relaxed, talking to Jeet, and I felt that I could talk to him freely. The way he talked added to the attraction I'd felt from our first meeting and made me like him more and more.

'Anyway, when I saw you and talked to you... Sorry. Please don't forget to remember me when you're free again, Rakhi.'

Jeet left and I didn't even say goodbye to him. I was wondering why he didn't finish his sentence or what he was going to say. He was in my mind the whole night. I felt he had stirred something deep inside me. I couldn't keep still. For a while, I paced up and down my room. That night I kept myself busy cleaning the house although it didn't need doing. I could not drop off to sleep because Jeet was in my mind all the time. Three questions were playing in my mind and I kept on thinking them over. Did he really like me as he said, or was he after one thing, as I had mentioned to him? Why was he interested in my life story? And why did he leave without completing his sentence? I didn't want

5

to raise any hopes for a relationship to develop in case I was disappointed and got hurt. It was still early days yet to say anything.

I must have dropped off in the end and woke up with the sun high in the sky. I panicked a bit, but fortunately it was still early for my clients. It was still ten in the morning.

I couldn't stop my work because I still had to earn my living. As previously arranged, I was about to entertain a client when I was surprised by an unexpected visit by Jeet. I was reluctant to ask him in. So I asked the client to leave through the back door, telling him that the caller was my cousin. I could have let him out through the front door, but I didn't want to fall out with Jeet. I think Jeet saw him, and I noticed a sign of anxiety on his face although he didn't say anything about it. That affected me a bit, and at that moment I decided to have a break from my work for a while. I welcomed him.

'Come in Jeet.'

'I'm sorry I troubled you yesterday,' Jeet said.

'You shouldn't worry about it,' I replied. 'It was nice talking to you. But what will your parents think when they find out that you've been visiting me so often?'

I was pleased when he said, 'Don't worry, Rakhi. I've been quite open with them and told them about my meeting with you. They don't seem to mind. Dad told me something ... can I be honest with you?'

'Go on, Jeet. I'm used to all sorts of talk. So don't worry. Go ahead and tell me what he said,' I asked, composing myself from the client's visit and the near-clash with Jeet.

Jeet reassured me that his father hadn't said

6

anything bad. One day when they were talking about me, his father had told Jeet that any man would like to be friends with a nice, pretty girl like me. (I am 5ft 5ins, medium build with black shoulder-length hair. I often got wolf-whistled when I walked around in my mini-skirts and high heels.) His father also told him that most prostitutes were pushed into the job because of the problems they had, especially as the result of broken marriages and money problems. Once they were in this job, they couldn't be trusted. They become hard-hearted because they'd learned to live the hard way. Some of those women reformed and became good wives and mothers depending on how understanding the people they married were. Some people even forgot that these women were human beings at all. His father had made it clear that they wouldn't know until they found the reason for me being in this situation. I was wondering how right his father was to think that way. It made me form a different opinion of his father and even of Jeet. But I didn't show him this.

I felt quite relaxed and willing to talk to Jeet. I agreed with his father's opinion about prostitutes and asked Jeet for his opinion about what his father had said.

'Well, Rakhi. I said that I wouldn't know until I'd found out from you.'

He went on to say that he worked as a qualified nurse at the Civil Hospital, the only general hospital in Port-Louis, and that he did his best to understand people and their problems.

'You see,' he added, 'I've done a course on psychology at the hospital. Using my knowledge of this, I'm able to judge people's character and the way they talk and behave. So, when I said you were in the wrong job, I had already formed an opinion about

7

you and worked out that you weren't what you claimed to be. I'm not an expert but I have that feeling. I may be wrong.'

'I was wondering how you knew I was in the wrong job from the short space of time you've known me, yet I didn't want to ask you. Now I know. I think I can trust you, Jeet. If you are prepared to listen, I'll tell you all about myself from the beginning. From that, you can tell me whether you're wrong or right in your opinion about me.'

'That'll be nice. And I don't care what anyone else says. This is just between you and me.'

'Would you like a drink?' I asked.

'If you've got it, a cup of coffee will do, thank you, Rakhi.'

Nurses were highly thought of. When Jeet said that he was a nurse, I got worried. He noticed it and wanted to know what the matter was. I said that I only had mugs and no proper cups and saucers to serve his coffee. I was quite relieved when he told me to stop worrying and that he was used to drinking out of mugs. So I made us some coffee and got some biscuits.

At this point, he said, 'Rakhi, please try to be yourself. I'm used to a simple life and I want to be like this whether I am nurse or a labourer.'

'It's just that I'm not used to welcoming people like you.'

'I'm no different from you,' Jeet answered. 'I'm only a nurse. The only difference is that I'm a man and you're a woman,' he joked.

'Ha! Ha! Anyway, make yourself comfortable,' I said. 'I hope I won't bore you with my story.'

'Don't worry, Rakhi, I'll tell you if I get bored,' he answered.

'May I ask you something, if you don't mind?'

'Yes, Rakhi. What is it?'

'Tell me, where did you live before you moved in here?' I was anxious to know.

Jeet was quite pleased that I asked him about himself. He started telling me that he was born and bred on the Trianon sugar estate, in the central region of Mauritius.

'Snap!' I said, 'I used to work on a sugar estate. I'll tell you about it later.'

'Oh?!' Jeet exclaimed and continued by saying that his mother and father used to work there as well. He didn't want to end up working with them. So he put his mind to his studies, no matter how hard it was to afford proper schooling in those days.

'Books were expensive to buy,' Jeet said. 'On occasions, we used to come to Port-Louis and buy books in a shop called the Corner House. Thank God, I got through my exams. My parents respect me for all the sacrifices I've made in order to be successful. After my exams, I could have gone into the teaching profession, but I didn't fancy the job. So I joined the nursing profession at the Civil General Hospital and I'm enjoying every moment of it. I got the urge to do nursing because when my grandfather was ill, we had a lot of problems finding a nurse to give him injections and advise us on medicines. Nurses were very hard to come by. So I joined the profession so that I could help others and understand more about diseases. My father developed a bad back and he could hardly do his job. They retired him on medical grounds after giving him a lump sum for long service. With that money we chose to buy a house in Port-Louis so that I could be nearer work, and to give us a change of environment.

9

'One of dad's friends mentioned this house,' he continued. 'It was going cheap as the man who owned it was getting too old to look after it. So Dad decided to buy it and then we moved in. Besides, it used to be a difficult journey to work for me. I had to change buses twice and most of the time I was late for work. They understood my situation and they used to let me off for being late. Usually they were strict with time keeping. Thank God we're all right now.'

'You must be brave to have made such a long journey to work,' I said.

To this, he explained, 'The Civil General Hospital was the nearest training hospital and I had to do it.'

'Now you've moved to Port-Louis,' I said, 'I hope you're settling in well now.'

'Yes, we're gradually getting used to it and the workplace isn't as far as it used to be. It's only about twenty minutes by bus and I'm always on time.'

'I hope you'll like it here. People are friendly, considering it's a town, not a village.'

'We hope so too.'

2

Life as a Youngster

'You've heard my story,' Jeet said. 'Let's hear yours.'

'Well! My name is Chitrekha – I was always called Chit. I use Rakhi for anonymity.'

'Oh?' Jeet replied. 'Chit is a nice name. Do you want me to call you that, or continue calling you Rakhi?'

'Thank you, but I think I'd like you to continue calling me Rakhi just in case you say the wrong name in the wrong place. I'm not shy of my name, but I'd like you to push Chit to the back of your mind.'

'Whatever you say. By the way, my name is Jeetendra. They call me Jeet for short.'

'That's a nice name as well. I'll continue calling you Jeet.'

'Whichever you wish.'

I began my story by saying that I was born in a small village called Barlow in the northern part of Mauritius. We lived in a three-bedroom thatched bungalow with an outhouse as kitchen and a pit toilet a few feet away from the house. We had large gardens in the front and at the back. Not too many people lived in the immediate area and we were almost surrounded by sugar cane fields.

When I was born, and having a typical Indian

11

way of thinking, my mother said she and my father were disappointed because they had wanted a son, So, they had to try again. I was quite plump and pretty and, as I was the first child in the family, I was spoilt to bits despite their desire for a son. I used to get all the attention and at the least murmur, I was picked up. I used to get all the toys they could afford. Mum and Dad used to take turns to look after me. In fact, I was never left alone. Everything changed when my sister Diya was born. Mum and Dad were disappointed again and had to try once more for a son.

I was two and I became jealous because attention was focused more on Diya than me. Whenever they picked up Diya I used to cry, but I still didn't get the same attention as before. When my sister Rena was born, I became used to the situation as I was three and had Diya as a playmate. I don't think my sister Diya felt the same way as I did, because she always had me as a companion. My parents were still not happy when another girl was born. My brother Deep was born when I was four. They were over the moon then, because they felt they had a complete family. Having a son was a pride for the family. It was just like hitting the lottery jackpot. I believe if they hadn't had Deep, they would have tried again for a son. Mum used to say that they didn't care how many children they had, they would have tried for a son despite the fact that they might suffer from poverty.

After Deep was born, they stopped having children. I don't know how they managed it. There was no family planning or contraception those days. That could have been one of the reasons why Dad became a drug addict.

My parents were labourers. My father was the third of four brothers. I never knew much about my mother except that she was an orphan and was living with an aunt when my father married her. She was from Goodlands, a small town further north of Mauritius.

Mum and Dad were happy working together at the same place. Mum said that Dad used to smoke occasionally, but later he became addicted to drugs – *ganja* – through a friend and became a different person altogether. Because of this, he left his job and took advantage of my mother, making her work hard in order to buy food and clothing for us. He used to take money from her and beat her up when he didn't have enough money to buy drugs. Mum couldn't tell her miseries to anyone. She knew that if she talked to anyone, it would get back to Dad and she would get beaten more. When Dad used to beat Mum up, we all used to get between them and scream to stop him going on. But instead of stopping, we got beaten up as well. The more we cried, the more he would beat Mum up as if, Mum used to say, 'a demon has got into him'.

We were scared of Dad because of the way he looked. He was tall and obese, with his stomach sticking out, and had a moustache. I think the moustache used to make us more scared of him than anything else. Mum was only of medium height and build. She wouldn't fight back because wives couldn't and wouldn't fight their husbands, no matter how much they got beaten up. I remember Mum having bruises on her arms and legs from being kicked and thumped, and Diya having slap marks on her cheeks. We couldn't say anything, but we used to massage Mum when Dad was not around. Mum used to feel pain in her arms and legs for some days afterwards.

We were frightened to approach Dad in case we got beaten, although he tried to cuddle us when he wasn't under the influence of drugs. Sometimes we didn't have anything to eat, but Dad didn't care about that.

Dad knew that my mother couldn't leave him because, being an orphan, she didn't have anywhere to go. The aunt she had lived with was dead by then. This was an arranged marriage and she had to put up with it.

My father wouldn't go to work yet he would entertain his friends at home and my mother used to cook for them. If there was no proper food, Dad used to swear at Mum in front of anyone, saying that she had offended his friends. It seemed that his friends used to enjoy this drama, because they would just smile and wouldn't say anything to Dad. So this meant that Mum had to work extra hours in order to provide us, Dad and his friends with proper food. Women usually worked Monday to Friday, from seven in the morning till one in the afternoon. Women used to earn less than men for the same hours of work, and I didn't think that was fair. Working extra hours meant that women worked until two o'clock in the afternoons, and on Saturdays as well. This set-up also meant that we couldn't go to school. My sister Diya and I didn't even go to primary school, and we couldn't read or write. Despite this, I had developed a talent of being able to talk and Mum used to say that I spoke 'like a great orator'.

'My second sister, Rena, and my brother Deep went to school, but their schooling was inconsistent. Some days they had to miss school because of the problems Mum used to have at home. We were children and too young to fully understand what was going on, but we soon knew when we didn't have food to eat or just had a cup of tea to go to bed on. Being the eldest child, I sometimes had a vague idea about what was happening. At other times, I didn't know what to make of everything. We were deprived of the chance to enjoy our childhood. We used to get jealous when we saw other children merrily going to school or playing around with their brothers, sisters or friends. We didn't have friends and no one could come to our yard. Whenever we were sent out for something and were late coming back, we were asked many questions by Dad about where we had been. In fact, no one used to come to visit us except, on occasions, for my uncles and aunt from Port-Louis. We also used to console ourselves when we saw youngsters going to work after they had been to primary school, and Mum said that those youngsters couldn't afford to go to secondary school. We stuck up for our mother. Sometimes she used to say, 'I hope you'll find true love when you grow up and that you won't have to go through this misery.'

We had little feeling for our father, because he never had time for us, except for the odd cuddle or more often thumps from him. We were always scared to approach him. Mum got fed up with all the demands from Dad and she was so desperate to lead a normal and decent life that she decided to live separately from him. She wanted to run away, but didn't know where to go. She had suffered for too long. One day she said to us, 'I can only put up with so much. I can't take it any more,' and Dad heard it.

He growled at her, and said, 'What can you do? Drown yourself? Go and do it in the river.'

She had to think about us, and her job. No one

would accommodate her on the spur of the moment with four children. In the end, she decided that she would look for a place to go to. She had heard that there was accommodation available at Camp Maçon (pronounced Masson and named after a yellow fruit that grew in abundance there), a village a few miles away that now no longer exists. She went and talked to the landlord, who I knew as Dada, and explained her problem. He was quite understanding and told her to move into one of his two vacant houses whenever it was convenient to her. She was surprised when he told her not to worry about paying him any rent, but she accepted the offer and decided to move in that same week, all five of us.

When Mum told Dad that she was leaving, he said to her, 'Go. See if I care. Don't bother to show your face here. Take these devils with you.' Meaning us. He also told her not to take a single piece of furniture, not that we had much, or anything else. Mum was very fortunate that the house was furnished, and Dada lent her some cooking pots and plates until she could buy some for herself. We children were excited at the thought that we wouldn't have Dad to shout at Mum or at us. We helped Mum carry as many clothes as we could in bags. Even my brother Deep, who was four, struggled to carry something. It was comical to see him walking fast with his tiny legs, but then Mum became emotional and said, 'There was no need for all these hassles of moving out. If it weren't for your father, we wouldn't have to leave our house to live somewhere else.'

On the way, we were making plans about what we would do, including Deep, who said in his own language, 'I'll help Mum cean ze-ze house and bing wata from za canaal, I will.'

'Oh bless him!' Mum said, with tears in her eyes. There was no tap water at the place where we were going. We had to fetch water from a nearby canal.

We were glad in a way that we had moved out because Mum didn't have to wait on Dad and his friends, nor did she get beaten up. At the same time, we weren't glad because, no matter how he treated us, he was our Dad and Mum's husband. Most people who didn't know what we were going through, called Mum all sorts of names for living separately from Dad, but she couldn't tell them the reason for it. The landlord was nice to us and gave us support wherever he could.

'Monee,' the landlord used to say to Mum, 'stay here as long as you like. If you need any help, don't hesitate to come to me or to my wife.' His wife was also nice to us and treated us as her own children.

We moved to a thatched house with two large bedrooms and a kitchen on one side of an open veranda, and a sitting area on the other. We considered this place to be adequate although we had to share rooms, especially as we didn't have Dad to bother us. We had a large playing area at the front and side of the house.

Mum now enjoyed a little bit of freedom. She thought it was bliss when Dad didn't bother her for a couple of weeks. Then trouble started again. Although Mum had moved out, she was still working at the same place. One pay day, she had a shock when she saw Dad waiting for her on the way home. She wanted to run away, but he had already seen her. He demanded money from her and threatened to beat her up if she refused. She got scared and had to give in to him. From then on, it became a habit for him to wait for her on pay days or when she was going to do shopping to the same village, the only shop for miles around. She didn't tell us about it in case we got scared, nor did she tell Dada. My three uncles knew what was going on, but they wouldn't intervene unless Mum wanted them to. Despite this, Mum was glad that she didn't have to cook for Dad nor for his friends. She wouldn't go to the police to report the *ganja* smoking and the threats because she didn't want him to get into trouble, for fear that he might do something worse in revenge. If she did that, she thought, it wouldn't look good for our reputation. He was our father. She would still not approach our uncles for help because she thought they had enough problems of their own.

Everything settled into a routine. I was ten. Mum was still giving money to Dad. Both my sister Diya, who was eight, and I were helping Mum with the housework and looking after Rena and Deep when they weren't at school.

When we were staying in Dada's house, an experience made me form another opinion of life. There was a couple living in another house. The only thing I knew about them was that they were Christians and that the husband's name was Gilbert. The husband used to drink alcohol quite often, usually every Friday when he got his wages. He used to beat his wife, and we used to watch them from our veranda. He knew we were watching them, but that didn't seem to bother him at all. Otherwise, he was a nice and friendly person. What I couldn't understand was that they seemed to forget they had had a fight the previous day, and used to walk about two miles to go to church every Sunday. This was probably the reason why the landlord didn't want to intervene in their private lives.

I used to wonder whether it was normal practice for people to beat their wives, but at the same time, wondered if that was the case, then why weren't Dada or my uncles beating their wives? I also wondered why a nice person like Gilbert turned nasty only when he took alcohol. After these experiences, I believed that alcohol and drug addiction could lead people to such behaviour. In the end, I developed a fear of this type of man and vowed that I would never marry someone who smoked or drank alcohol.

Dad wouldn't go to work and, because he smoked heavily, his health started to suffer. He developed a very bad cough and became ill with a chest infection and had a high temperature. Mum felt sorry for him and went to see him.

'I've come to take you to see a doctor,' she urged him.

Dad turned nasty towards her and said, raising his voice and struggling with his intermittent cough, 'Go away! Why have you come to bother me now? I've told you not to show your face here. For me, you're dead. I don't want you to take me anywhere. Let me die alone.'

Mum felt like saying, 'I wasn't dead for you when you wanted money from me', and, 'Where are your friends when you need them?' Instead, she said, 'I'll take you to see a doctor because you're not feeling well.'

'Go away,' Dad said furiously. He accused Mum of having an affair with Dada and also of trying to arrange marriages for us with Dada's children. He tried to get up and hit her, but he was too weak to get out of bed on his own. He fell out and nearly banged his head against the wall. Mum had to virtually wrestle him to put him back to bed.

Despite this, Mum took us to see Dad. At first I wasn't sure whether he was pleased to see us, until I noticed tears in his eyes. We were still scared to approach him, yet we kissed him.

The next time we went to see him, he said, 'Come and give me a cuddle before I go.'

Dad was especially bad when he was on drugs. Now that he couldn't take drugs because of the condition he was in, he was shaky and delirious, yet he often managed to throw scorn at Mum. He wouldn't even let her wash him. So Mum had to call one of my uncles to help her. Dad mellowed after my uncle talked to him, and became grateful that Mum insisted on looking after him, yet he insisted that he wouldn't go to see a doctor.

It wasn't easy to find a doctor those days, especially in Barlow. It was even more difficult to go to a hospital. The nearest hospital was at Poudre D'or which was about 15 miles away. The distance seemed even longer when we went by bus. To get there, we had to change at Rivière-du-Rempart, and the roads weren't so good. The buses were slow. Mum could have taken Dad to the local health centre – the dispensary – but because consultation there was free, there was always a long queue. So Dad wouldn't have gone there in his condition because he hated queues. Besides, the nearest dispensary was based at Rivière-du-Rempart, which was about four miles from where we lived. We had to go there by bus as there were only a couple of cars in the village and they were too expensive to hire. A doctor used to come to the dispensary every Tuesday and Friday.

Dad remained stubborn. His condition worsened and he eventually died of pneumonia. Before he died, Mum told us later, Dad apologized for his behaviour and said he was grateful that Mum stayed by his bedside till the end.

I can't say whether we were glad that he died. His death might have been a shock to Mum, but we didn't understand death. We were told that he had gone somewhere, and we were under the impression that he would come back and that we could have our occasional cuddles from him. I expected Mum to miss him, because she had been married to him for the last 15 years. I think she was pleased in a way that Dad had died because of the way he had behaved as a husband and father. Yet Mum used to cry, although she tried to avoid crying in front of us. If she did, we used to cry with her.

I wondered if we would go back to our own house. Dada, the landlord, being sympathetic as usual, told Mum that we could go back if we wanted to. We thought she didn't want to go back yet because if Dad came back, the problem would start again.

'Dad wanted to kiss us before he went,' Deep said to Mum, 'so he's coming back.' It took a lot of convincing to make us believe that people didn't come back when they died.

Mum told us she preferred to stay where we were, and said she would go back when everything had settled down. At least for the time being, she said that we were happy where we were staying. In the meantime, Mum had asked my youngest uncle, Sona, who was staying in a rented house, to move into our house if he was willing to. He could look after the house and tend the gardens.

'I would like you to plant some flowers in the front to make the place look nice,' Mum said to Uncle Sona, 'and grow some vegetables at the back. You can do this in your spare time and continue with your job as usual. Please, please, I won't take any rent from you.'

Uncle Sona was single and only too happy to look after our house. Mum used to visit it and do odd jobs now and then. She continued with her work as usual and was glad that she didn't have anyone to harass her or pester her for money. She became her own boss and this was evident by the way she asked Uncle Sona to do things. She couldn't do that when Dad was around. Now we could have proper food (and no starving on occasions) and clothing. We could wear clothes that Mum couldn't afford to buy for us before. Rena and my brother Deep could continue with their schooling without interference. Mum was also glad because she said that she could live a decent life, without the bruises and aches and pains which she received when Dad used to beat her up.

Mum worked for the next few years and then decided to extend the house, adding two more bedrooms with a concrete roof instead of thatched, before we could move back. We were all excited that we could have a room each and arrange it our own way. Mum gave the spare room to Uncle Sona, who was still single. We were pleasantly surprised that he had reserved a space in the back garden for us to play in, and to invite friends to play with us.

Mum continued to work as a labourer on the Antoinette sugar estate, also known as Phoolyaar, which is where Indian immigrants had first settled as slaves in the nineteenth century. The estate belonged to a landlord of French origin. Mum had worked there for some years. On odd days she used to take me with her to help so I was earning something which helped her with our expenses. On other occasions, I looked after my brother and sisters. Later, when I was 15, the employer took me on full time. Some people would have seen this as child labour, but it wasn't considered as such then. Once someone looked grown up, they would be employed, but on less pay than the women. It was also cheap labour, which wouldn't happen these days.

I didn't find working in the field very hard because I had become used to it when I was accompanying Mum before. The work in the field was seasonal: cleaning ditches and gleaning for canes after canes were freshly cut, or planting new canes at the beginning of summer and cleaning the cane ditches to make it easy to cut canes during harvest time in winter. I didn't like the winter job that much because I had to wrap my arms and partially cover my face despite the Mauritian heat, usually above 20° centigrade, to avoid cuts from the razor-sharp sugar cane leaves or friction from the tiny needles on the cane stems. These could cause itchiness and irritation to the skin. However, Mum was pleased with the extra income I was earning because she said that we would be better off. She also said that when Uncle Sona left, we would have the house to ourselves and then she could have a decent proposal for my wedding.

As I was young and good-looking, men were always interested in talking to me. Sometimes they used to disgust me. So I always used to talk to them in such a way that they never used to bother me again. Mum praised me for my attitude, and she used to tell us to speak our mind in order to defend ourselves. If we didn't, we wouldn't get anywhere in life. She used her life as an example, as a way of getting through the miseries of life. That's the way I learned to speak out and get on with my life. Besides, I've always been chatty, and Mum used to tell me that I was an early developer.

After Dad passed away, Mum was not entitled to a pension. In those days, most people used to get married through a religious ceremony only. A registry wedding wasn't so common. In the case of Mum being an orphan, a religion-only wedding took place after it was arranged by relatives. So, I supposed she wasn't entitled to anything. When it came to sharing properties, husbands used to marry their wives through a procedure called affidavit, and children took their name as a result. I don't think Dad had done that either. Besides, I wasn't sure whether he himself owned the property legally or not. He was too busy entertaining his friends in the end, and he never had the time to sort things out. We were hoping to find out who got what when the land was shared. I was hoping that Uncle Sona had some knowledge about it.

Mum used to say that Uncle Sona was no problem. He could continue to stay with us if he wanted to. We got on all right with him and he was helpful to us. It wasn't that she was using him, but he was helpful around the house. Some people were under the impression that she wanted to marry him. However, I was certain that Mum, being a widow, wouldn't make the same mistake twice by marrying someone else, especially the brother of her ex-husband. Besides, marrying a second time was against the Hindu religion and he was much younger than her.

Uncle Sona respected Mum and he always called her 'sister' instead of *bhabhi* (sister-in-law in Hindi). One day he approached Mum and said to her that he had lived long enough at our place and that Mum

24

hadn't taken any money from him towards his keep. He was quite happy living at our place and that we got on well with him as he did with us. But he said that we were growing up, and that Mum needed more space for herself and us. It was about time he got himself a place and moved out as she might need some privacy.

'Sona,' Mum replied, 'you've lived with us for so many years. We like you being here and I'm sure the children would like you to stay here as well. It's me who asked you to move in here, and I'd like you to stay. You talked about privacy. You're part of the family, Sona. When you're here, we feel safe. I wouldn't ask you for rent – you're not a stranger. So don't worry about it. I don't want anything from you. If you think you have to go, please feel free, but I'd like you to stay with us. Please don't feel that we're stopping you. If I need space, I'll have another room added to the house.'

I was surprised that Mum wanted uncle to stay when he could've gone and minded his own business elsewhere. In the end, we were glad that he decided to stay and continued to help us wherever he could. I suppose he knew how bad Dad had been towards us. He always gave us presents on special occasions like the New Year, except for birthdays which we never celebrated.

Life continued as usual without any problem until one day Mum said that she would like to marry me off so that I could start a family of my own and, if possible, continue to help my brother and sisters. I was surprised at her suggestion, especially as I was working and helping her towards a decent life. I hadn't expected that suggestion and I didn't know how to react to it. At the time, I disliked the idea, although I suppose most girls of my age would be dreaming of getting married and starting a family of their own. I also thought that most girls would have liked to live a better life than working in the sugarcane field.

Instead, I was annoyed and said, 'What! Have you had enough of me? Do you want me to be treated like you or like Gilbert's wife?'

Mum tried to reassure me that she hadn't had enough of me, and that not every man was a drug addict or alcoholic. She added, 'No Chit, I only wanted you...'

'To get married and start a family,' I interrupted her. 'No, Mum, the way I feel at present, we are a happy family. I don't want any misery added to my life. So I don't want to take any chances and get married yet. I have to see to the welfare of my sisters and brother first. I'm too young to get married. I'm only sixteen.'

To this, Mum replied, 'Don't worry about the children, Chit. I've coped all my life and I think I can cope now. We can find a nice boy for you. You're beautiful, and we won't have problem finding someone to suit you.'

'I know you can cope, Mum,' I replied, 'but I can also see that you're not the same person as you were few years ago. You're getting on. You get tired easily and most of the time you're out of breath when you do extra work. God knows how long you can keep up with your work at Phoolyaar.'

After this talk, she agreed to relax a bit and decided that I could help her for another year or two before thinking of my marriage. Then I could not refuse. She was concerned that if a girl didn't get married by a certain age, people would think that something was wrong with them.

I told her, 'My dreams have been broken by my bad experiences of Dad and from Gilbert. I don't care what people think. I wouldn't mind staying single if it comes to that. Also I know, Mum, how my brother and sisters have suffered in order to live a decent life. Do you think I can forget them? So I'll tell you when I'm ready, Mum.'

'Whatever you say, Chit!'

I could see Mum was slowing down. I couldn't tell whether it was due to the hard work she had done all her life, or to her age. I couldn't say how old she was because, being youngsters, we couldn't ask her age.

One day, when I was eighteen, Mum fell ill with a chest complaint. At first I thought that she would get well quickly, but then I thought of Dad, who also had a chest complaint and died as a result. One consolation was that Dad smoked heavily and Mum didn't. The pain continued and Uncle Sona advised her to take a household remedy, to drink boiled mint water in case she was suffering from upset stomach. That didn't help. In fact, the pain got worse and she developed a persistent dry cough and experienced discomfort when breathing. Uncle Sona was ready to help. He decided to take Mum by bus to see a doctor in Desforges Street, in Port-Louis. I had to stay behind to look after my brother and sisters. When the doctor examined Mum, he told Uncle Sona that she was suffering from a chest infection, and prescribed her some antibiotics. My uncle paid the doctor his consultation fee and bought the medicine from a chemist with his own money. We started Mum on the course of antibiotics as soon as she came home.

As I was old enough to understand the situation, Uncle Sona told me about Mum's illness, but asked me not to tell the children in case they got worried. I was supposed to tell them that Mum would get better with the medicine she was taking.

Uncle Sona stayed up for the best part of the night and gave Mum whatever she needed. It was just as well, because Mum's condition worsened during the night, which Uncle Sona thought was due to the medicine she was taking. We couldn't seek advice from a nurse or a doctor about the medicine, because there was none available in the area. We also thought that Mum's condition could have worsened because of the travelling she had done by bus, 15 miles each way to Port-Louis. The long walk to the doctor's surgery from the bus depot hadn't helped her either. I became panicky and didn't know what to do to help. I was asking if she wanted a hot drink one moment, and the next moment I was asking her if she wanted a hot water bottle. I was also trying to massage her legs. Mum couldn't say what was hurting. So I asked the children to help massage her as well, whilst Rena rubbed coconut oil on Mum's head. With all this going on, Mum became emotional and we had to reassure her that she would be all right. Uncle Sona urged me not to panic too much because it wasn't good for Mum.

We had to rush her to Poudre D'or hospital by car because she couldn't bear the pain in her stomach. Luckily, someone in the village had a car and didn't hesitate to take Mum to hospital although we had disturbed him late at night. I had to stay behind again for the sake of my brother and sisters.

They spent several hours at the hospital, Uncle Sona told me later, while doctors did some tests on Mum. I felt sorry for the car owner. Luckily, he was self-employed and didn't have to rush back home.

After the tests, they found that she had cancer of the stomach in its advanced stage. This meant that they couldn't do anything to save her. Uncle Sona was told that, if they tried to operate, she might not recover from it and might die. The doctor who examined Mum at the hospital also told my uncle there was a chance that Mum only had a few days to live. He gave him the option of either admitting her to the hospital so that they could look after and give her a large dose of painkiller, or taking her home and giving the painkiller there so that she could be with her family. Uncle Sona talked to Mum about her condition, saying that the doctor had advised her to have a complete bed rest and that she had the option of staying at the hospital or going home. He was careful not to tell her that she had cancer. With the anxiety on my uncle's face and the way she felt, Mum knew that something was wrong. So she preferred to come home and be with her children. I was surprised that they were able to diagnose Mum's disease and give such an answer so quickly.

It occurred to us that the first doctor didn't know that Mum had cancer because he hadn't done any tests or X-rays on her, whereas the hospital doctor did. The diagnosis of chest infection was bad enough, but the news about cancer was devastating. I didn't know much about cancer. When Uncle Sona explained to me that it was a disease that ate people inside until they died, I said to myself, God, why does it have to happen to Mum, especially after what she has been through?

I was reassuring my brother and sisters, telling them that Mum would get well, and trying hard to hide my emotion, knowing that we would lose our

29

mother soon. I was reassuring myself that we would be all right, yet I was thinking that when Mum died, I would have the responsibility of looking after my brother and sisters. Uncle Sona said that he would look after us, but I realised that things wouldn't be the same without Mum.

My sister Diya was 16. Although she was old enough to understand what was going on, I still considered her to be my little sister – naive and innocent. She asked me a few times if Mum was going to die. I told her not to be silly, not to think like that. Rena, my next sister, was 14, and my brother Deep was 13, and I considered them to be too young to understand anything. In fact, they never asked anything after I reassured them that Mum would be all right after taking her medicine – painkillers and a sedative to help her sleep. I felt I wasn't protecting my brother and sisters enough, especially after the treatment we had had from Dad. People might say that they were being over-protected, but I didn't think that way. Besides, I thought that was the way children were brought up in those days, because I was. There were things we could tell them and other things we couldn't.

I continued to work at Phoolyaar, and Diya was looking after Mum because I used to tell her what to do in my absence. She seemed to be coping well. I told the people at work that Mum wasn't well, and some of the women came to visit her on the way home from work.

At first, Mum was taking food little by little, but later she couldn't eat at all, although we mashed the food for her. We had to give her teaspoonfuls of water. She became very weak and could only talk faintly.

When she was dying, she said something that has stuck in my mind. She said to me in a nice clear voice, which surprised me, that 'They are going away. I have to go now.'

I asked who 'they' were, and said, 'There is no one here.'

She said once more that they were going away and then died with a jerk, turning her head the other way. Her body went limp. I believe the 'they' she referred to were some kind of celestial beings. It was scary.

I was still holding her hand, but then I tried to hug her, screaming and saying, 'Come on, Mum, speak to me, please, please. Say something.' I became hysterical, not knowing what to do and who to turn to, because Uncle Sona had taken the children for a walk as if he knew that Mum was going to die. I wished they were there so that Mum could have seen them before she died. I was still crying and holding Mum when Uncle Sona and the children walked in. I left Mum and ran to hug the children and my uncle, screaming and crying, 'She has gone. She has left us.'

All the children started wailing with me, and Uncle Sona did too.

Soon uncle calmed down and straightened Mum's body and, covering her with a sheet, went to tell his brothers. On the way he told the neighbours, and within minutes the house was full of people with everyone trying to console us.

My aunts bathed Mum and then clothed her in a white gown. They laid her on one side of the room and covered her with a white sheet except for her head, so that people could see her face. About 50 men and women kept vigil during the night. And

31

there was Mum lying peacefully as if she would wake up any moment and talk to us.

Later I found out that people with cancer usually show some signs, such as losing weight or hair. As for Mum, she was on the plump side and she stayed like that until the end, and she kept all her hair. It was probably the reason no one suspected her disease. We didn't tell anyone and no one guessed she had cancer. The only thing that happened was that she became yellow a day after she came back from the hospital. I was told that that could have been the result of a test they had done on her liver. From this test they found out that she had cancer. It was only after they interfered with her liver that she became yellow – like she had jaundice, and made everyone believe that this was what she died of.

All my uncles were involved, informing relatives and friends of Mum's death. Mum was cremated the next day. It was the saddest day of my life. All the people assembled in the front of our house when Mum's body was placed in her coffin. She still looked as if she was sleeping. It was the last time we saw her face, and it drew a fresh fit of crying from us. Then the coffin top was put in place and nailed down. The coffin was lifted and carried away, followed by men only. My brother, sisters and I became hysterical. I don't know where all the energy and tears came from – we were all crying. All the men – women weren't allowed – carried the coffin on their shoulders the two miles to the nearest cemetery, where Mum was cremated. Later, Uncle Sona reassured us that Mum was resting in peace. We held a ceremony in her memory the same evening. That was when I got to know some of our relatives, who reassured us and promised to visit us often. Most of the relatives, including an aunt from Ste Croix, told us that we could visit them any time, and this aunt gave me directions how to get to her house which I remembered visiting with my parents when I was younger.

I lived for the sake of my brother and sisters. I was sad, but after one week at home I had to go back to full-time work at Antoinette for our survival. I didn't want to leave my brother and sisters on their own, but Rena and Deep had to start school. So I took Diya with me to work, to earn some extra money. At work, everyone sympathized with me, and that used to make me sad. At times, some of the workers used to help me when I was behind with my work. They all said how nice Mum had been. Even the foreman used to tell me to take it easy, and tried not to give me much work to do.

My role had changed. Whilst Mum used to work to buy food and clothes for us, now I had to work for this reason. I worked really hard so that I could provide for the needs of my brother and sisters. Now I realised how hard Mum used to work in order to provide for us, and she had Dad pestering her for money for his enjoyment.

I guessed Uncle Sona had talked to my other uncles, because they came to see us one evening. The eldest uncle talked to the four of us and said that I had been working really hard and they felt that they would like to help us out.

He went on to say, 'Chit will get married soon and Uncle Sona will be left to look after the three of you. I don't think it's fair. Your father was our brother. So we've discussed the problem among ourselves and have decided to adopt you as our own. Your cousins, our children, would like you to be among them. We cannot take you all together, but

33

as we live in this small village, we can each have one or two of you. We'll let you think about it and let us know who wants to go with whom. Of course, you can come to visit your home whenever you like.'

I could have told my uncle that I was happy to look after my brother and sisters, but because it concerned me getting married, I preferred not say anything. I didn't intend to get married, but I didn't know what could happen in the future.

We, my brother and sisters, had a talk among ourselves because I thought it was nice of my uncles to make such an offer. At first none of them wanted to live apart, but when they thought about how hard I had to work for their keep, they decided to go. Rena wanted to go to my eldest uncle, Diya wanted to go to my second uncle, and I preferred to stay at home with Uncle Sona and keep Deep with us. After making such a big decision, all four of us embraced, promising that we would never lose touch with each other no matter what happened to us.

The uncles came back two days afterward. I told them the decision and everything was settled.

My eldest uncle said, 'I'm glad that you made such a decision. If you like you can come with us now, or come another day. Remember that you can come and go here any time you like. We promise you that you'll be looked after well. Chit, we don't want anything from you. You have enough on your plate already.'

Everyone decided to go then, and start a fresh life. We all embraced again and were in tears before everyone left. It was a heart-breaking moment to see everybody leaving, especially as it wasn't long since Mum had died. I felt bad about Dad, thinking that if he hadn't smoked heavily, he would have been alive to look after us as a whole family. Mum wasn't there, but at least he could have kept us together. However, I told myself, what had happened couldn't be undone. That was life and we had to continue living it, no matter what befell us.

I stayed awake for most of the night. I was worrying that being the eldest child in the family, I had failed to protect my brother and sisters. It was the custom for the eldest son or daughter to look after his or her younger brothers and sisters if they lost their parents. When the eldest child is too young, as I was, uncles and aunts take the responsibility until it is no longer required. Maybe I could have managed to look after them, but now anything could happen. I couldn't stop crying that night, and I had to go to work in the morning.

I carried on working, hoping that I would contribute towards the welfare of my sisters although my uncles said that they wouldn't need any help from me. Everything was running smoothly. Then I had to think about my future as well. Uncle Sona wanted to help me.

3

Marriage Proposal and Courting

It was about six months after my mother had died, and I was just about getting over it. I was still working at the Antoinette sugar estate, but I didn't have to work as hard as before because I only had Deep to look after. As for Deep's school fees at the college, Uncle Sona had volunteered to pay. We had to pay in those days – every month, in advance, and by a certain date. If the payment was delayed, students were sent back home until the fees were paid. So some children missed out in that way.

Mostly, I used to walk alone to work – about a mile – and sometimes I was accompanied by other workers. I had to walk through lanes, some muddy and others full of overgrown grass. The lanes had tall sugar cane plants on both sides when it was nearing harvest time. I used to wrap myself up to protect myself from the sharp sugar cane leaves, and walked with my working boots along the lanes, which were especially muddy when it had rained.

When, sometimes, I used to walk along those lanes and it was quiet and there was no breeze, it felt quite eerie, as if someone might jump out and pounce on me. I had heard tales that thieves hid in those areas and attacked passers-by to rob them. I wasn't

36

scared of robbery because I didn't have any money or jewellery on me, but I was scared because I was a young girl and someone might attack me.

One day, a young man stopped his bike and said he wanted to accompany me to work. I didn't feel scared because I knew him – he was from the same village and worked in the same estate, doing a different job. But I was nervous in a way, because I didn't know what was in his mind.

Sunil, which was his name, said he hoped I wouldn't mind him talking to me and accompanying me to work. In those days, young girls weren't allowed to talk to young men, unless they were related. It was worse being in an isolated lane, which would give the girl a bad name. If they were seen talking, people in the area got to know it and that could ruin the chance of the girl getting a suitable person to marry her. In my case, I didn't mind because, as I had said to Mum, I didn't care if no one wanted to marry me. I didn't want to get married and end up being beaten like her. I also didn't mind because people in the village knew my situation. It was known that in villages everyone knew everybody and everybody's business. A village was just like a family unit.

Sunil walked me to work and then rode off to his own work. This attitude made me feel safe in his company. On the way, he talked about things in general, mostly village gossip and how brave I was to cope on my own. I usually don't like it when people gossip, because it shows that they don't have anything better to do. I didn't mind him talking about my parents, but I was trying to avoid conversation on the subject as it always made me sad.

At that time I didn't know whether he was talking

to me this way just for the sake of it, or if he was just trying to involve me in conversation as I was reluctant to talk to people I didn't know well. I had to accept what he was saying, but at the back of my mind I held the fear that he might attack me one of these days. He accompanied me on several occasions and one day he said that he liked me. That increased my fear of him attacking me. I went into a daze for a moment. I didn't take seriously what Sunil had said because I thought he was joking. The fear of being attacked made me say that I liked him as well, because I didn't know what he was likely to do if I didn't reply to him this way.

Then I thought that he must have liked me, to accompany me to work – but I didn't know what his intentions were. In those days, some people believed that liking someone meant the same thing as loving someone.

Anyway, Sunil couldn't accompany me back from work because he finished later than I did. Some days when I was on my own, I looked forward to his company because I had someone to talk to in those lonely lanes. He always found something to say, although most of the time I didn't know what to talk about. I couldn't talk about television programmes as there was no television in those days. I couldn't talk about films because I couldn't go to the cinema – there was no one to take me. He was always talking to me about films he had seen, how he liked certain actors and actresses, and his favourite songs. I used to listen to him with eagerness because everything was new to me. He said that all the films he had seen were musicals and were based on romance.

One day when I walked home from work, I saw Sunil's bike in front of our house. He was on the veranda talking to Uncle Sona and drinking tea. I knew my uncle was on holiday that week but I didn't know Sunil was.

So I asked him, 'Aren't you at work today?'

'No,' Sunil replied. 'I had to do some work at home. So I took a day off. Knowing that Uncle Sona was at home, I came to talk to him.'

'If you had taken time off,' I reasoned, 'you should be doing what you ought to be doing instead of wandering around.'

He said, 'I know,' and left. I sensed that something was in the air by the way he left.

Later, when I was resting, I asked Uncle Sona what Sunil was up to.

'Chit, may I talk to you?' he asked.

'Yes, of course, Uncle,' I said. 'What's the matter?'

'Chit, I think you understand that I've tried to look after you and Deep as your parents would have done. I'm also trying to advise you what's best for you. Now you're getting older, I think it's about time you started thinking about your own future. Your mother had talked to you about it, and you had said that you were too young to get married.'

'Uncle,' I said, 'you know that Mum has just died, and she's still fresh in my mind. At this moment, marriage is the last thing I'd think of. My sisters are living with the other uncles. They are always at the back of my mind and, as a sister, I have to see that they are fine, although I know they are being well looked after.'

'Chit,' Uncle Sona interrupted, 'you can't grieve all your life!'

'Uncle,' I shouted, 'she was my mother and you don't know what it's like to lose a mother at my age.' I started crying.

'Chit,' Uncle Sona said, trying to calm me down, 'I've lost my parents as well, and also a lot of other things to be in this situation.' That shut me up, and he continued, 'You have to think about yourself and your future. You get married and have a family...'

'And be beaten up like Mum?' I interrupted. 'Besides, you know how poor we are. To find a decent proposal for marriage, as Mum used to say, is difficult. People know that Dad used to smoke pot and that Mum and Dad are dead. They'll understand that, being on my own, I lead an unusual life, especially when I go to work on my own. They won't understand that I work so hard to make ends meet. I know you're helping us for which I'm grateful. They'll try to...'

'Hang on, Chit, hang on,' Uncle Sona interrupted me. 'I understand what you're trying to say. You know Sunil was here this afternoon. He was telling me how much he likes you. He said that he thinks you two have a lot of things in common. He wanted to know if you'd like to marry him.'

When I heard this, I went quiet. It was as if I had been struck by lightning. For some reason, I went temporarily in a daze. When I came to my senses, I wondered if this could be the love Mum had referred to, which she said would brighten up my life. Yet I told Uncle Sona I was surprised Sunil had come up with such an idea. I told him I hardly knew Sunil, and that he had started accompanying me to work two weeks ago. I stressed that it was too soon to say we had a lot of things in common.

'I bet he says this to all the girls he meets,' I said.

'I wouldn't know, Uncle Sona replied. 'But that's what he told me.'

'I like Sunil,' I said, 'but it doesn't mean to say

that I love him or want to marry him. There is a big difference between liking and loving someone. I think Sunil is a nice person. He likes to talk and tell jokes, but I don't really know what sort of person he actually is. He is from the same village and I think it is too close for comfort. Besides, according to the custom, it isn't he who should have come to propose. His parents should have approached you.'

I was surprised at my newly acquired courage. I was now talking to Uncle calmly, despite being upset a moment ago, and although he was older than me. He had always talked to me openly in the past, and it was possible that I was taking advantage of that. Usually, people in Mauritius, especially girls, didn't talk to their elders like that. I remembered that Mum had told me to speak up for myself and realized that was what I was doing. I was being brave, and I suppose that I was like this also because I was on my own, and I knew Uncle Sona respected me for that.

Uncle Sona said Sunil was aware of the fact that he shouldn't be approaching him. But he had wanted to find out what I would say through Uncle. Then he intended to ask his parents to come to see me at our house. Uncle Sona reminded me that he had known Sunil for a long time. He appeared to be a nice person, and no one in the village had said anything bad about him.

Then my uncle said something that made me change my mind. 'Imagine,' he said, 'if it were someone from a different place – you wouldn't have known him, his personality, nor his likes and dislikes. Here you've met Sunil, talked to him, and you know something of him. What else do you want?'

I told Uncle Sona there was logic in what he said.

41

I would let him deal with the situation, although I was not so keen on getting married yet. He thanked me for my reply, and said he was not forcing me into getting married. He wanted me to make a future for myself, despite him not having the chance to do so. I told him I had often wondered why he never got married, but I had never dared ask him in case I offended him.

'You wouldn't have offended me,' he said. 'Remember when I said I had lost a lot of other things? Well it concerns my personal life.'

Uncle said he loved someone in the village. She used to work at the same place as him. They knew and loved each other for over two years. They thought that nothing could separate them. They vowed that they would never get married to anyone else. It was a blow to both of them when her parents wanted her to marry someone else. Uncle Sona couldn't go to her parents, as the custom went, and suggest he marry their daughter. His own parents weren't alive to approach her parents. He couldn't approach his older brothers, because he was too shy and didn't know how to. It would have been pointless for the girl to tell her parents. It wasn't the custom for the girl to choose who she wanted to marry. So, in the end, they married her off to someone else. Uncle Sona was sad and vowed that he would never love anyone else. She was his first love and he didn't want to allow anyone else near his heart.

'Surely she's happy and well in her life. Do you ever get the chance to see her or talk to her?' I asked him.

The girl had been married for seven years and, on occasions, she stole a few minutes to come and talk to him whenever she came to visit her parents.

She didn't have any children, and said that she wasn't happy with her marriage. She felt like killing herself, but she had to keep afloat because of her parents and their pride.

'Sometimes I feel like running away with her. But I cannot do it because I think of my pride and of my brothers' and sister's reputation. I have not talked about my grief to anyone. Honestly, Chit, you're the first one to know about it, even though so many years have passed. Whenever someone asks me why I never got married, I just shrug and tell them that I'm not interested.'

'I'm sorry about this,' I said. 'I really feel bad for you. I won't ask you who it is, despite you having said you still see her.'

'Although I trust you, Chit,' he replied, 'I'm sorry, I won't be able to tell you who it is. It's a secret I won't reveal to anyone. I always think of her and pray to God that He would work some miracle for us to be together.'

'Let's hope,' I tried to reassure him, 'that God will help you. Put your faith in Him.'

He looked sad, and I saw tears in his eyes. He changed the subject to my dilemma. He said that I had a future, and a choice of whether or not to marry Sunil. He continued by saying that I didn't have to worry about my brother, because he would persuade Deep to continue with his studies at his expense, so that Deep could be a credit to our name. He said, 'Who knows what he'll become one day. We hope that he won't end up like your father. Only fate will decide. I hope he'll follow a good path.'

The mention of Dad's name made me angry. I would never forget his attitude toward Mum. I thanked

43

Uncle Sona for what he was doing for us, and said I would go along with what he thought was best.

'Don't thank me,' he replied. 'Thank your mother for allowing me to help you. Anyway, I'll talk to Sunil and see what he comes up with.'

Sunil couldn't talk to me the following day because I was accompanied by other workers. I met him the day after, which was a Friday. I started a conversation with him about something different, hoping that he would say something about his meeting with Uncle Sona. He didn't even raise the subject. We talked as if nothing had happened. Before he left me at work, he said that he was coming to see me on Sunday with his parents.

'Rat!' I said to myself. 'At least he could have said something to me. Why doesn't he take things seriously for a change!'

I took it that the matter was being dealt with by Uncle Sona. I couldn't call Sunil back because he had already disappeared. I couldn't go back home to ask Uncle Sona what it was all about, because I could be late for work. I was angry because I had thought that Uncle would never have made such arrangements without talking to me. Surely he would have told me about it. In a rage, I kicked the ground, nearly slipping and falling down. I was fuming and cursing both Sunil and Uncle Sona for keeping me in the dark. I wasn't happy, especially when I was still grieving.

Even at work they noticed the difference in me although I tried to contain myself. One worker asked me if I was all right. 'I'm sorry,' I replied, 'I'll be all right.' But I couldn't stop thinking about it. I couldn't concentrate.

As soon as I came home, still fuming, Uncle Sona

said that Sunil had come to see him the previous day. Sunil told my uncle he had talked to his parents, and they were coming to see us on Sunday. Uncle Sona was sure we were free on Sunday afternoon, and so he invited them for about two o'clock. He also apologized to me for inviting them without asking me first.

'I don't mind,' I said to Uncle Sona trying to contain myself, 'so long as you know what you're doing. It would have been nice if you or Sunil had told me about it. I spoke to him this morning and he didn't say anything about talking to you. I was mad.'

'I couldn't tell you because you had already gone to work when I got up this morning. So, I take it that's settled,' he said. 'I think we must invite my brothers to see what opinion they form from this meeting. What do you think?'

'I don't know, Uncle. I leave it to you.'

'I'll tell them, as they are our elders, or else they will feel left out.'

On Sunday only one uncle came, because the other had to go somewhere else. In the afternoon we were relaxing on the veranda after our meal when Sunil, his parents, and another man who I later found out to be his brother-in-law, came at 2.30 p.m. with a present which they gave me.

They sat on the veranda, which was quite spacious and served as a lounge. I addressed the parents as Uncle and Auntie, as we did to all the people in the village who were older than us. We asked them if they wanted anything to eat. They didn't want anything and so I made a cup of tea for everyone and offered some cakes I had baked.

During tea, Sunil's mother started the conversation.

At first, she complimented me on the cake, and then talked to me about my work and how we were coping without Mum and Dad, and how my sisters were getting on with the help of my uncles.

Then she turned to the uncles and said, 'I think you know why we're here and I'm sure Chit knows as well. We've been urging Sunil to get married for some time and he hasn't been giving any thought to it. He keeps on saying that he isn't ready to get married yet. We keep on telling him that he has to settle down sometime because we can't look after him all the time. He's our only son and the only daughter, who's older than him, is married to Kavi,' she said, pointing to Sunil's brother-in-law. 'We've been to see several girls for Sunil and he keeps on telling us that he doesn't like them.'

It occurred to me that choosing girls was like choosing tomatoes in a market. I would have preferred to see a love marriage allowed for a change. Uncle Sona's story made me think that way.

'Anyway,' his mother continued, 'for two weeks now he's been saying that he likes Chit, and that he wants to marry her.'

I noticed that they used the word 'like'. Uncle had also said that Sunil liked me. There was no mention of love from anyone. I was wondering, how can a person *like* someone for two weeks and want to marry them? It seemed to me that he was infatuated with me, whereas I didn't have any feeling for him.

His mother continued, 'When he mentioned marriage, we grabbed the opportunity and wanted to act on it. Chit,' she said turning to me, 'we know your background and we understand that children aren't to be blamed for their parents' mistakes. We've known your father, Nund, and your mother, Monee, for a long time. We also know that you're a hard-working girl and we think you'll make a good partner for Sunil. Would you like to marry him? I know you won't say no to us...'

Everybody's eyes turned on me. It was just like sitting in front of an interview panel, where everyone was waiting for a reply from me. I didn't know what to say. I didn't agree to the proposal straight away. I didn't say much at the time because I was thinking of this 'liking' business. Everyone eventually left, saying that they hoped to receive a positive reply.

I talked to the uncles. Even my other uncle reassured me that Sunil was the right person for me, and he left when I told them that I'd try. 'Try? It's not a matter of trying,' he said. 'It's the question of yes or no or rather of your life.'

'All right, Uncle, I'll go along with it.'

My sisters came to see me the following evening and they, together with my brother, agreed that I had made a good choice in Sunil. My three uncles met Sunil's parents the following Sunday – I wasn't supposed to accompany them to Sunil's house – and told them that I had agreed to marry Sunil. It was like opening a floodgate. Sunil started coming home every day and having meals with us. We got on well. Most often we used to talk about ourselves and how we would plan our future once we got married. Sometimes I could tell from his conversation that he was not mature enough to act his age. It was a boyish love. At that time, I couldn't do much about it because I wasn't that experienced myself. I thought things might change with time.

On occasions, he used to take me to the cinema at Baroda picture house in Rivière-du-Rempart. We started talking about films we had seen, and eventually

47

we talked about the actors and actresses we liked best, and the songs. Our conversation centred around films, actors and songs – nothing about ourselves. Later the cinema burned down – I heard that it was a case of arson. We couldn't go to see films unless we travelled long distances. So Sunil bought me a Pye radio so I could listen to songs. At least I had something to talk about. At other times, I used to hum my favourite songs.

On other occasions we used to go to Pamplemousses Botanical Garden, where we used to walk along avenues of coconut trees, past lakes and beds of many different flowers. I used to enjoy looking at the large water lily leaves with their occasional flowers in one rectangular small lake, which was one of the tourist attractions in the garden. It was a romantic feeling. But whenever I went out, I used to tell Uncle where I was going because I felt he was still responsible for me until I got married. Also, whenever we went out we had to take my sister Rena or my brother Deep with us as a chaperone, because we weren't allowed to go out, even to the cinema, on our own before we were married. It was still fun. Sunil used to take me shopping on Saturdays, because most shops were closed on Sundays, and buy clothes for me. He got on well with my brother Deep and sometimes he used to bring sweets and presents for him.

I grew fond of Sunil and I looked forward to seeing him. Sometimes I made plans about how I would arrange things in my new home. I thought that I had found the love I had been searching for. I was learning to be happy again, especially after the death of my mother. Sometimes Sunil used to take me to his house, although I wasn't supposed to go there, and his mother would cook nice meals for me. I started calling her 'Mum'. I got on well with her.

One Sunday I met his sister, who was nice to talk to. She was expecting her first child and she was telling me how much they were looking forward to it. 'I hope it's a boy.' I was surprised that she had the same attitude as my parents had, but I went along with her, saying that I also hoped it would be a boy. She also told me how she and Sunil used to spend their childhood playing different games. I couldn't tell her about me, because I didn't have such luck.

Although I was getting married to Sunil, he didn't mind me continuing to call him by his name. It was thought to be improper and unrespectful to call husbands by their names – wives called their husbands by the Indo-Mauritian term *uho*. Uncle Sona was pleased that I was finally happy, and so were my two sisters, my brother and my other uncles. Uncle Sona kept them informed of any development with my relationship with Sunil.

We couldn't stay overnight together while we were courting, because this never happened under our customs. We always had a chaperone. And the 'like' I was concerned about earlier was becoming love. We were becoming impatient, and promising each other that we would never stray away from each other. All we wanted then was to get married so that we could stay together all the time, instead of going our separate ways after a day out.

4

The Wedding and Married Life

A family reunion was held before proceeding to the wedding itself. It was decided that we wouldn't hold the usual engagement ceremony because it would incur extra and unnecessary expense to both parties. It was also decided that the wedding would take place a year and a month after my mother had died – when I'd be nineteen. Sunil's parents decided to build a separate two-bedroomed house in front of their existing house so that we could move in as soon as we got married. His mother and father would continue to stay in their house and entertain their relatives there.

After these decisions were made, preparations were in full swing. My aunts helped me buy my wedding clothes. It was kind of the uncles to buy food and other items we needed for the wedding. As for the invitations, it was decided to let Sunil's parents invite the people in the village, partly by word of mouth and partly by cards. My uncles preferred to invite our relatives as well as their close friends from the local and neighbouring villages. In fact, everyone in the village was invited. This was because we knew everybody and we would have felt guilty if we had left someone out. When I told people from work that I was getting married, each one was pleased for me and wished me luck for the future. Most of the time they were talking about me, about my mother, and my hard-working nature. I also became the talk of the village, especially as I was getting married in the same village.

We were both looking forward to this big day when we would be together, planning and doing things together. Sunil told me that his father had a surprise for the day which he wouldn't tell me about, nor did he give me any more hints. I was excited to see what that surprise was.

Before the wedding, I was given a month's holiday from work so that I could prepare myself for the big day. During the wedding week, some men got themselves busy pitching a tent in front of the house in order to accommodate about one hundred guests. If one belonged to a village society, members usually came and did this work. We had two types of clubs in the village. One was where people of the same religion went. We also had a club where people of different religions used to go, and the members were mostly youngsters who got involved in sports and other activities. My father didn't belong to any of these societies when he was alive and so there were no members to help us out. So my uncles had to ask their friends to help with pitching the tent. From Tuesday onwards some village women, who were invited by the aunts, came in the evenings and prepared food ready to be cooked during the wedding weekend. After this preparation, the same women got involved in singing and dancing sessions till late into the night. It was fun. When I said 'weekend', I meant Friday to Monday. Most relatives started arriving on Friday with a view to helping out, and didn't go back home until Monday afternoon.

On Saturday, other relatives started arriving from early afternoon. Records, a record player, and a loudspeaker were brought in by a person who acted as a disc jockey for the weekend. In no time, music was playing at full blast. It was so loud that we could hear it for miles – but no one would complain.

At six o'clock in the evening, a minor ceremony, one of a few pre-wedding ceremonies, was held after which guests were served meals at one side of the tent. On the other side of the tent singers and musicians were adding fun to the night. They were involved in an event similar to karaoke. There was a harmonium player and a drummer. Village singers were trying to compete with each other in songs – some folkloric and others rearranged film songs. I couldn't tell who was the winner. After that, music was started at full blast. As for me, after the first ceremony I was smeared with saffron, especially on my face, arms and feet. This ritual indicated the purity of the bride-to-be. During this session, some women tried to tease me by putting saffron in my mouth. When this was completed, I was left in my corner with my sisters to keep me company. I had to stay there until the morning, when I was to be bathed by some female relatives before I was prepared for the wedding. The blaring music stopped at about one in the morning, giving the relatives (and me) the chance to have a rest wherever they could – in the spare rooms and in the tent. The music started again at eight the next morning with everyone trying to liven up.

The wedding day was good. God blessed it with a sunny and pleasant day. The wedding was due to take place at twelve o'clock. Some people were busy preparing and decorating the area – *bedi* – where the actual ceremony was to be held. I couldn't see any of it because some female relatives and friends were busy preparing me. I was ready by 11.30 a.m. and I was told that I looked radiant in a red sari (girls always wore red saris to get married in, to signify purity) with henna on my hands, feet and forehead and a lot of gold chains and bangles given by my uncles as a present for the wedding.

As the time was approaching, I didn't know whether to be sad or excited. I was sad because I could see my brother and sisters watching every move I made. I was excited because I was going to start a new life full of hope and expectation.

It was 12.30 p.m. and there was no sign of Sunil's party. They were late. Mauritians are always relaxed and are never known to be on time for an appointment. Hence the term 'Mauritian time'. At 12.40 p.m., the music on our side stopped and all I could hear were cymbals and drums being played a few yards from our house. My brother Deep ran to tell me what was happening. He had seen an ox decorated with flowers and little bells round its neck. Even the reins were decorated. The ox was pulling a cart covered with nicely decorated sheets. Sunil was dressed in his white wedding gear and looked great. Instead of sitting next to his brother-in-law (who was the best man) in the cart, he was playing cymbals and dancing and singing with the village group. His father was sitting cross-legged opposite his brother-in-law. His guests, instead of taking cars, preferred to walk behind the singers because Heera lived only about a mile from where I lived. Only men were allowed to accompany the groom, and the women customarily had to stay behind to prepare to welcome the newly-weds later – unless the wedding was taking place in a rented hall where both men and women could go.

It was a lovely and entertaining show which I had never seen before. It was like a fairy tale. Sunil told me later that was the surprise his father had thought of, and he wouldn't tell me beforehand as it would have spoilt the fun. I didn't know whether to laugh or cry when my brother told me that Sunil was singing and dancing in his wedding gear. In fact, I was so overjoyed that I cried, thinking that Mum and Dad would have liked to see this. The pre-wedding ceremonies of the two groups were completed, with Sunil's father and his guests meeting my eldest uncle (standing in for my father) with our guests on the road, women welcoming the groom, and Sunil and I exchanging garlands.

Eventually the main wedding ceremony started at one o'clock. At the beginning, everything went all right. The priest delivered his speech, talking briefly about my parents, welcoming the guests, and congratulating Sunil and me for this big day and wishing us a lasting and happy life together. The saddest part was the moment when my eldest uncle and aunt had to give me away to Sunil. I couldn't help crying because I kept thinking that it was my mother and father's responsibility to give me away. I had to be comforted by my other aunt who was sitting next to me as my assistant on the *bedi*. Eventually, I calmed down and the wedding was completed after forty-five minutes.

When the wedding ceremony ended, we went into the house where the last wedding rituals were carried out. In the meantime, guests from both sides were served food in the tent, after which the majority of the guests went home because they had to catch a bus and the bus service wasn't so frequent.

It was send-off time. At this moment I felt sad again at leaving behind my brother and sisters, because I felt that my responsibilities from then on weren't to them, but to my new family. My home was at Sunil's. I reassured Deep that Uncle Sona would look after him and that he should continue with his studies for his own good. I also reassured my sisters that I would try my best to visit them. Besides, I realised that at my new home, some of my freedom would depend on Sunil. I was still crying and being comforted by my aunt. It was time for us to climb onto the cart, using a set of makeshift steps.

We sat cross-legged. I sat with Sunil on my right and my escort – this was my aunt from Ste Croix – sat on my left. It was the custom to send a lady escort with the bride for the night, to give moral support to the bride on the first night at her new home. Sunil's brother-in-law and father sat opposite me.

On the way back, the singers and dancers continued to entertain us. Sunil couldn't join them because he had to stay with me. When we reached Sunil's house, we met some women, including his mother and sister, who were waiting for us at the entrance. They welcomed us with a garland each, after which we went into our newly built house. The house was completed only a month before the wedding, and I had helped Sunil to buy and arrange the furniture and everything in the house. At the door we were stopped by some female relatives who wouldn't let us enter until Sunil gave them money – a teasing game played by the groom's relatives. I don't think Sunil had expected that, so he had to borrow some money from his brother-in-law to give them. We entered the house and, after another short family ritual, we changed into casual clothes and both of us went to meet his relatives who had stayed behind.

On the first night we had to sleep separately because we had relatives around. I slept with my escort by me as well as some female relatives, and Sunil slept in the next room. It was just like sitting in my corner on the night I had the saffron on me.

The following day, we got ready in our best clothes and went to our home in a car which was hired for the day. This time the women went as well. Everyone else preferred to walk. I was greeted by my brother and sisters. We had a meal, met friends and relatives, and left late in the afternoon, leaving the lady escort behind.

Overall, it was a good wedding. Everything went smoothly. After that day, everything and everybody settled into a routine. I didn't have much of a problem getting used to married life because I got on well with everyone – except that I couldn't decide what was best for me. Being a woman, I had to agree with Sunil, and most of the time he decided for me.

It was time for me to return to work. After Sunil and I discussed it, I went back to work only three days a week. All my colleagues welcomed me back but they said that I shouldn't have gone back to work because Sunil was there to look after me. In fact, Sunil didn't want me to go back to work at all, but I insisted that I'd do it so that we could save some money for a rainy day. We had decided that I would work part-time for two years and then give it up altogether.

I used to visit my brother and sisters and have

meals with them and they used to visit me and have meals with us quite regularly.

We used to go to the Luna Park cinema at least once a month in Port-Louis, as the Baroda had burned down. We also went to the seaside quite often – without a chaperone. I quite liked going to the north-eastern coast at Poste Lafayette, which had a long stretch of white sandy beach. I liked digging in the sand until I found water. When the tide was low, I would walk for a few yards into the sea with Sunil by my side. The water was pleasantly cool and I felt like staying there for ever especially when it was warm on the beach. Sometimes Sunil and I liked to walk along the beach and watch how our footsteps were swept away by the incoming tide. At other times I liked to lie down under the filao trees and enjoy the cool breeze from the sea. That used to make me fall asleep and wake up fully relaxed.

It was bliss. It was like heaven on earth. It was best when there weren't too many people on the beach, because as most people used to picnic there or cook meals on makeshift burners, they used to play football or other games and make lot of noise. Unfortunately we couldn't stay there too late because, as we didn't have a car, we had to rely on public transport and had to catch the last bus at five to come home.

In fact, we were rarely at home on our days off. We were either visiting friends and relatives, or going on trips. Sunil's mother used to say that nothing got done around the house. Whatever spare time I got, I made it a habit to help Sunil's mother with the washing and cooking. Some days we used to cook and eat at her place, and at other times I used to cook and either invite his mother and father for dinner or share the food with them. We got on very well. His mother used to tell me stories from her past, which I found fascinating.

Sunil and I always had our meals together. Whenever he was late coming home, I used to wait for him. He would come home, gave me a kiss and a hug, and then we ate. We became very close. One day when we were at the Curepipe botanical garden, he said that he would like to spend many more days like that together. 'You know, Chit,' he said to me, 'I think we won't have children for another few years so that we can spend more time with each other, instead of tying us down with them just yet.'

'That sounds great. We won't, then,' I replied. 'But we have to explain this to Mum and Dad so that they won't get worried about our health. They might think that we've some problems and that we can't have children.'

We both talked to Mum and she agreed to our decision, although she felt sad that she wouldn't see her grandchild for a while.

'You must explain the situation to your uncles, Chit,' Mum said. 'I'm sure they would like to know your decision as well in case they too get worried.'

'I'll do it, Mum,' I replied. 'I think they are as understanding as you are.'

Two years of our married life passed by as if nothing was going to separate us. I was 21 and Sunil urged me to stop working. I thought it was a blessing in disguise. Everyone at work was sad to see me go. Because I wasn't working, I started putting on weight and most people asked me if I was pregnant. Going on a diet wasn't recognized at that time nor was controlling our eating habits. So I continued to put on weight.

My sister Diya was almost 19 and was engaged to marry a man in Flacq, a small town in the east of Mauritius. Rena was turning 16 and was just completing her School Certificate examination, similar to GCE 'O'-level, set by Cambridge University in England, and Deep was in Form Four (the fourth year at the secondary school).

All of Sunil's relatives liked me and they enjoyed coming to visit us and chatting to me. I thought I had found the love of my life, and that it would continue to strengthen. I remembered that my mother used to say I would find my love one day, and I thought that this was it. Everything was going smoothly for me, when there was a change...

5

A Wind of Change

I thought Sunil and I were very close and very much in love and that I was everything to him and he was everything to me. But my suspicions were aroused when one day he was late coming home from work. Thinking that he had met some friends on the way home and was delayed because he got chatting, I waited for him for tea. Instead of coming home at four, he was still not at home at six. When he came in at half past six, he didn't apologize for being late, nor did he tell me the reason. Thinking that he could be tired from working overtime, I didn't ask him anything in case he lost his temper. At the same time, I thought that he would have told me if he was working overtime. I didn't want him to feel that I was restricting his freedom and not giving him room to move. Besides, I thought this was one of the things that happened. When he came in, we had our usual kiss and hug, he had his wash and we had our tea, as always, together.

He was not late for the next few days, but he was the following week. I still didn't ask him anything. I didn't want to be too hasty in drawing conclusions, as it might turn out to be a storm in a teacup. It gave me cause for concern when he came in late twice the third week and he didn't kiss me. I thought I would ask him what was keeping him late at work.

'I suppose you were working extra hours? You must be too tired to give me a kiss,' I asked.

He was elusive and just said, 'I think you can put it that way,' and didn't say anything else after that, apart from giving me a quick kiss and no hug.

He was making a habit of being late two days a week. One day I said to him that he could at least have told me that he was going to be late coming home.

To this, he raised his voice and said, 'Look. I don't have to tell you when I come and go in this house.'

His tone of voice stunned me, especially when he had been so nice to me before. I didn't know whether he was serious or not, yet I said to him calmly, 'I'm only asking you so that I won't have to wait for you for tea.'

'Don't ask me anything and don't wait for me. I told you that I'm working late. What else do you want to know?'

I was shocked. He didn't say a word to me that evening. He didn't have anything to eat later, and went to bed with his back turned to me. I didn't know what had happened all of a sudden. I was nice to him as usual, and he was turning nasty towards me. Now I knew that this was serious.

One day, his mother asked me about Sunil's late homecoming. I told her that he was working late. 'That's funny,' she said, 'I've never known him to work that late!'

'Well, Mum,' I replied, 'if he says he's working late, he's working late. I have to believe him.'

'Believe what you believe,' Mum replied, 'but I still find it odd.'

The lateness increased and I didn't feel like asking him anything. He was coming home late and sometimes wouldn't bother having his supper. He just used to wash, put his pyjamas on and go straight to bed. I tried to talk to him, but only got 'yes' and 'no' replies. I didn't say anything to his parents because I thought that might make matters worse.

At first, I thought he was drinking alcohol and thought of the way Gilbert from Camp Maçon used to treat his wife, but I couldn't smell it on his breath. I also thought that he might be mixing with drug addicts. This reminded me of the way my father treated my mother. But there was no sign of this either, because Sunil never even smoked a cigarette. I was becoming confused. I had the urge to go and find out where he went after work. I couldn't do it because it wasn't an easy task for a woman. I had thought about it, but then I realized that if he found out, he might be furious. He might think I was spying on him. Besides, I didn't know where he was working, and also he always went to work on his bike.

His mother came to see me one morning and said, 'Daughter, I can see that things aren't the same with you. Is something bothering you, Chit? Are you ill or what?'

'Nothing, Mum. I'm fine, thank you,' I replied.

She didn't ask any more questions. Sunil's attitude was becoming worse. It was driving me crazy because he wouldn't tell me what was going on. He went away one Sunday morning when we were supposed to be going out. I got ready and waited for him, hoping that we would go out when he came back. There I was waiting for him, all dressed up and having had nothing to eat. He finally came back at six o'clock. By this time, realizing that we wouldn't be going anywhere, I had changed back to casual clothes and prepared dinner. I asked him where he had been when we were supposed to be going out.

'I forgot,' he said. I dished out dinner and served him. He scoffed it without waiting for me. I still didn't lose my temper.

I said to him, 'You forgot that we go out on Sundays? You've not forgotten it for the last few months. Please, Sunil, tell me what's going on. You've not been yourself. Aren't you well or is there something that's bothering you?'

'No. I'm all right and nothing's bothering me.'

'What have I done wrong that you can't tell me about? You can tell me. I won't mind.'

'I told you. There's nothing wrong. For goodness sake! Would you stop asking me questions?'

'Sunil, we've been married for over a year and I thought that we were getting closer day by day. I also thought that we would discuss any problem that comes up. What's wrong, and what are you keeping from me?'

All the time I was talking to him he wasn't looking at me, as if he wasn't listening to me. Then he said, 'Look. I'm tired. Let me go to sleep. I have to work in the morning.'

I couldn't say anything to him after that because he was asleep in no time. I sat on the edge of the bed for some time, thinking about what to do to make my marriage work. In fact, I couldn't do anything because I didn't know what was wrong. I got into bed and he had his back turned to me. I felt like running out screaming, but I resisted.

6

The Last Straw

The routine of Sunil coming home late and sometimes not coming in at all went on for a few weeks. I was often ignored as if I were an alien in the house. One day I determined to know the truth about Sunil's problem.

'Please, please, Sunil,' I said, 'tell me why you're treating me like this. We were getting on so well and all of a sudden this happens. I've got feelings as well, you know.'

To this, he replied in an angry tone, 'If you really want to know, I'm seeing this woman from Amaury.' This was a village a few miles from where we lived. 'Her name is Mala. She's a nice lady and I like her a lot.'

He used his favourite word 'like' again. When I heard this, I was dumbfounded and stood staring at him like a statue. I couldn't talk and I couldn't cry. I just stood there. When I came to my senses, I ran to the bedroom and sat on the edge of the bed for the whole night. He didn't bother to follow me. I think he stayed in the lounge for the night.

In the morning, I felt weak and drained, and my eyes were red and puffy from crying and lack of sleep, but I still prepared his breakfast as usual as if nothing had happened. I couldn't eat anything. I prepared and packed his lunch as usual, which he took with him. I presumed he didn't want anyone to know that there was something wrong, and I didn't want anyone to know either.

I was wondering where I had gone wrong. I had tried to give Sunil all that he wanted, but I was wondering how come Mala suddenly became 'nice'. I wished I could bring him back to me. But I didn't know how to. My mother had said that I would find the love of my life. I was wondering whether this was that love, or had it just been an illusion. I was deep in thought when, at about ten o'clock, Sunil's mother came to see me.

'Chit, may I speak to you? I didn't see you around so I came to see you. I thought that you might be busy doing something. God, you look awful.'

I thought to myself that it was Sunil she should be talking to. He was her son, but she didn't know what was going on. I also wondered if she wanted to talk to me because she had become closer to me than Sunil for the last few years, or because she thought it was her duty to talk to me.

'Yes, sure, Mum,' I said.

'Please tell me if there's anything wrong between you and Sunil. I can sense that something is not right.'

'Honestly, Mum, there is nothing wrong.'

'Chit, I'm your mother-in-law and I'm a friend to you as well. Whatever you say, think that you're talking to a close friend. Last time I asked you, you said that there was nothing wrong between you and Sunil. When I asked you now, you still deny that there was something wrong. There must be something. You look pale. You've lost weight and now your eyes are red showing that you've been cry...'

She couldn't finish her sentence because I was crying uncontrollably. She hugged me and said, 'Some say that crying your heart out makes you feel better. So, cry it out.'

I didn't want to cry but I did. Then she said, 'Come and sit down and tell me what's the matter.

I told her what happened the previous night and everything Sunil had told me, hoping that she wouldn't get me into trouble. Instead, she was shocked and said that she couldn't imagine why her son was acting like that.

'There you are,' she said, 'I told you that was odd, didn't I?' I nodded.

She said that she would talk to Sunil later and that she wouldn't say that I had spoken to her. 'I don't think I'll bother his father,' she said. 'You see, he works odd hours and sometimes on night duty at the orchard, where there are lots of fruit trees. He has to walk around the orchard in case people come to steal fruit at night. Because his work is dangerous, he's given a licensed gun to carry with him in case he's attacked. I manage to see him for few hours and then he has to go back to work again. So I don't want to worry him in case he has a bad night thinking about Sunil's behaviour. You see, his father doesn't behave like this. He's the nicest person I've met.'

This was the first I knew where his father worked, and that he worked 'odd hours and at night'. So that was the reason why he used to be in bed most of the time, and that we didn't see him for days on end.

Sunil's mother said that she would talk to his father if it was really necessary. After urging me to have something to eat, she left. I promised her that

I would eat my food for her sake and that I wouldn't do anything silly.

Sunil turned up late that evening. I don't think Mum saw him come in, because in villages people went to bed by nine o'clock at the latest. There was no television and nothing to stay up for. Sunil came in and we had our dinner together without him saying a word. He went to sleep. Because my mind was restless, I wanted to talk to him.

'Sunil,' I said, 'are you asleep?'

He said bluntly, 'I wouldn't have answered you if I was sleeping, would I?'

'I suppose not. I just want to know about this Mala. Where did you meet her and how long have you been going out with her? I'm concerned. Your mother came to see me this morning and asked me if there was anything wrong between us. I didn't want to tell her anything because I thought I would try to patch up my marriage.'

At the mention of his mother, he sat up and said, 'Look, Chit, I told you not to ask me questions, but since you mentioned Mum coming to see you this morning, I can only tell you that Mala used to work in the same place as me. She was married and is divorced now. She lives on her own and wants me to move in with her.'

I didn't know whether he was saying all these things just to make me jealous or if it was a true story. If it was true, I couldn't do anything about it – I couldn't confront her, nor could I talk to him to make him change his mind.

Then he added, 'I'll talk to Mum when it's convenient. For now, I think we should separate on a trial basis.'

For a moment I was dumbfounded, and then felt

like strangling him, but I said, 'Where do you think I'll go? I don't want to go to my family house or to my uncles. This is my house. What will my uncles say? How would my brother and sisters feel? Think of my pride. People will laugh at me. You won't get any blame for it. You're a man. They'll blame me although I've not done anything wrong.'

I didn't know who the blame would fall on, but I was sure it would be me, because women always got the blame. It was the same when my mother had left my father. No one blamed Dad because they didn't know his faults. No one would blame Sunil.

'I won't ask you to go anywhere,' Sunil continued. 'You can stay here. If you don't want to stay here or go back to your home, I don't care where you go, but go. I don't care what people say.'

'Sunil,' I said, 'what happened to all the sweet talks we used to have? What happened to all the promises we used to make? Don't you think anything of them?'

'I don't care about those things. Promises were made to be broken. You're annoying me now.'

'No, I'm not,' I replied.

He went to hit me, but stopped himself. He yelled, 'Get out of my sight! Get out of here!'

This reminded me of the time when Dad told Mum to get out and never to show her face there again. I nearly said to Sunil that he would have cared if my uncles had confronted him. I ran to my bedroom. I didn't sleep a wink the whole night. He went into the lounge and I could hear him snoring in no time. I didn't know how he could just sleep, carefree, when my mind was in turmoil. I sat up on the edge of the bed the whole night. In the morning, I made his breakfast and packed his lunch for work, although I couldn't bear to look him in the face because of the way he had treated me the previous night. Yet I said, 'Sorry about...'

It seemed that my voice was irritating him. He didn't let me finish my sentence before he said, 'Go away. Don't talk to me', and snatched the lunch box and dashed out of the house without having his breakfast. I wondered why I had prepared his lunch, but I had thought it was my duty. He left so early that his mother missed him, unless she had decided she didn't want to bother him until later.

Mum came round again in the morning and asked me how I had got on last night. I just told her that there was no change in Sunil's attitude. Sunil didn't turn up that night or the night after. I was boiling with rage and felt that if I knew where Mala lived, I would go and drag him out from there. Now I was desperate to do something. I wanted to talk to Sunil's mother, but I didn't think she would be able to solve the problem. I couldn't turn to my uncles or aunts because they already had the responsibilities of my brother and sisters. I couldn't allow my brother and sisters to come to my home in case they found out about my problem. Besides, I wasn't in the mood to welcome anyone.

I didn't do much for the next few days. I couldn't put my mind to doing anything. I was always thinking about what had happened. Whenever I tried to do something, I went into a daze.

I found that I was almost running out of food because Sunil wasn't shopping as often as he used to. I didn't have much money to buy anything as I wasn't working. I wouldn't be able to go to ask my uncles for help unless I told them what was going on. I was approaching a breakdown.

Sunil's attitude was becoming worse. I asked him for some money the next time he came home. He threw some rupees notes at me, telling me to buy some food. He made me feel that I was begging from him. When I told him that he shouldn't be throwing money at me like that, he tried to hit me for the second time. He lunged at me but missed. At this point I remembered I had told Mum that I wouldn't get married because I didn't want to be beaten up. So I decided this was the last straw because, first, since Dad's beatings, no one had ever tried to hit me before. I remembered how Mum got beaten up and we all got slaps and punches from Dad when we tried to stop him. If I had mentioned this to my uncles, they would have killed him for that. Secondly, I had never been shopping and I didn't know where to start. Uncle Sona had always done the shopping for us.

Sunil was nasty. His Mum came to see me as usual and saw me low in mood. She said she wished she could help me. She was going to buy some things from the shop and asked me if I wanted something. I said that I didn't want anything, and so she left.

I knew she was going to be out for quite a while because she liked talking to people whenever she went out. When she left, I started thinking. I thought that it was pointless to suffer in silence. I didn't want to act silly and contemplate suicide. I had to think fast. I also had to think of the reputation of my family. I didn't want to stay there and be beaten up. My mother had sought and found refuge when she was going through hardship. She was grateful for Dada's kindness which helped her manage to solve some of her problems. Besides, I myself have worked very hard and managed on my own. I didn't want to spoil everything and do something silly. So I had to do something before my mother-in-law came back.

7

In Search of Love

I was fed up with everything. I couldn't stand the treatment I was getting from Sunil. His love had turned sour and he couldn't stand the sight of me. He had got himself a girlfriend to replace me and he found her to be more attractive than me. He had asked me to move out or try a separation on a trial basis. He threw money at me as if I was begging from him. As a last resort, he tried to hit me. I was scared that this could lead to the kind of severe beatings my father gave my mother, or Gilbert gave his wife.

I remembered my mother's words, 'I cannot take it any more'. I didn't think anyone could, or would. I wanted to leave everything and run away somewhere. Suddenly I thought of my Aunt Savi, my father's sister, who lived in Ste Croix, a place in the east of the city of Port-Louis. She had always wanted me to go to her home and I decided I would seek refuge there.

I quickly packed some of my clothes and a few other things I might need (anything, at random, because I didn't have time and I was in no mood to think) into a couple of *tantes*. (These are carrier bags woven with special leaves – there were no plastic

72

bags in those days.) I took the money Sunil had thrown at me and went to catch the bus for Port-Louis. I didn't see many people around as most of them were working or busy with their housework, and luckily there was still no sign of my mother-in-law. On the way, I made sure that I didn't show any sign of tears or distress.

I was fortunate to catch a bus as there was no set timetable. I paid my fare to Ste Croix. I could vaguely remember where my aunt lived because she had given me the directions several times. But in my state of mind I couldn't remember the name of street where she lived. What if I got lost and had to ask someone for directions? I had an idea of its whereabouts. In order to get off the bus near her home, I had to look for a police station on the right after a certain bridge. In order to be certain of the place, I had asked the conductor to tell me when we reached it. I got panicky when I saw one police station on the right. I couldn't remember seeing a bridge until the conductor told me that it was Terre-Rouge.

The bus reached Ste Croix and the conductor reminded me where to get off by showing me where the police station was. I got off at the next stop and it seemed that I was in a different world. I had been to my aunt's place before, but that was when I was very young. I stood at the bus stop wondering which way I should go. I couldn't ask anyone, because whereas in the village we talked broken Hindi (Bhojpuri), in Port-Louis they spoke broken French (Creole or patois) which I was not very good at.

I was praying to God to give me courage, and to help me with my problems. Being in a strange area on my own was different from being with someone and also having been given the directions verbally was different from seeing the place. I was pacing up and down, and a few people tried to offer me help but I still couldn't remember the name of the street. They could tell that I was a country girl by the way I was dressed. I realized that town people dressed and behaved differently from country people. I was like a dumb person because, when they asked me where I was going, I looked at them vacantly, not knowing how to reply to them in Creole. I couldn't ask for directions for my aunt's home by her name because I only knew her as Savi. This didn't mean anything to the people there. In the end, I had to cast back in my memory, although I could hardly think straight. After thinking hard about which way to turn, and searching for her place carrying my three *tantes*, I eventually managed to find my aunt's house, with a mango tree in the open yard – the others were fenced off. Fortunately, my aunt was in, my uncle was at work, and her three children were at school. She welcomed me and talked to me over a cup of tea.

She asked, 'How come you came alone? Where is Sunil?'

'I've come alone, Auntie,' I replied. 'We had a row and I left home without telling anyone where I was going.'

Her face lit up at the mention of me leaving home. Then I told her everything that had happened between Sunil and me. I ended up saying that I hoped she would help me until everything settled down.

Then she said, 'I'm sorry about your problem. You shouldn't have left without telling anyone. It's not ladylike. Does it mean that you aren't going back?'

I started crying. I was surprised that she wasn't very sympathetic. Her attitude toward me was different from what I knew from before. I was wondering how she would have felt if she was in my shoes.

I couldn't reason with her as she was older than me, but I said, 'I don't know, Auntie. I thought that I would spend a few days with you. It'll give me time to cool down and to think things over. Anyway, I couldn't stay there and be beaten up like Mum.'

'So you are following in your mother's footsteps, living separately from your husband.'

'No, Auntie, it's just that I don't want to be beaten up.'

'I'll speak to your uncle when he comes back from work and see what he's got to say. I don't think he'll mind so long as you're prepared to go back in few days. In the meantime, you can stay with us. I'm sure you'll get on with the children because they know you and you know them.'

The children came home from school and they didn't have any problem with me. Uncle and Auntie talked to me the same evening and both agreed to accommodate me for a while. Uncle was a quiet type of person. It was my aunt who did most of the talking. After a week, she approached me and asked what my decision was.

I said to her, 'Auntie, I've been through a lot. I can't go back and face the same problems. I might end up killing myself. If you don't mind, will it be all right if I stay here until I find myself a job and a place to live?'

She agreed to accommodate me so long as I started looking for a job and a place to stay. She stressed that I couldn't stay at her place forever.

Living in a city after living in a village all my life

wasn't easy. After one week, I had already experienced some of the city's lifestyle, although it was very different from the village. By now, I was getting used to the language because Auntie's children always talked to me in Creole. In the village, one could always find someone to talk to. Everyone knew each other. Here, we sometimes didn't know who was who. Most people minded their own business and they didn't have much time for anyone else.

Auntie knew that I would find city life different from village life. So she let me familiarize myself with the place for the next two weeks. Because Ste Croix is on the outskirts of Port-Louis, she showed me where to catch the bus to go to the city and where to get off. She accompanied me on two occasions. Being a woman didn't help, because I wasn't supposed to walk about just for the sake of looking around. It wouldn't make much difference if I were a boy, as everyone might wonder why a girl was walking about. Yet, I tried to walk about. I had one incident. Port-Louis has so many streets that I got lost one day. I had gone into a supermarket, and when I came out, I didn't know whether to turn right or left. I walked a few yards both ways and still couldn't retrace my steps. Usually, because I couldn't read, I had a landmark, such as a building or a sign, to follow in case I got lost, but this time I didn't see anything to follow. Finally, I remembered which door I went through in the shop which meant that was the way I came in.

It seemed that I was being regimented, with a timetable to find work. At the beginning of the third week, my aunt wanted me to go out and look for a job. She also offered to accompany me to some interviews. She lectured me on how to find a job.

She asked me to go to restaurants and supermarkets and ask if they had anything to offer. At the same time I could ask those people if they knew of any accommodation for rent.

I didn't seem to be getting anywhere with my search for a job or a place to stay. I didn't know whether it was the way I was expressing myself or the way I was presenting myself. I was still unable to speak Creole properly and I was still not dressing myself as a town girl would do.

At the start of the fourth week, the problems started. When I came back from an unsuccessful interview, feeling disappointed and down, Auntie said, 'Chit, I don't think that you're trying hard enough to get yourself a job. You should put your mind to it so you'll be successful at interviews.'

'I know what you're trying to say, Auntie. But you know that I don't have much experience with the city lifestyle and I don't know how to approach these people.'

'Chit,' she said, 'you don't need experience for a cleaning job. You don't need experience to work as a domestic.'

'I know, Auntie. Wherever I go, they ask me what experience I've got. I tell them that I don't have any experience except that I have worked on a sugar estate.'

Auntie laughed at me, as if she had better experience than me when she first got married in Ste Croix. That annoyed me a bit, as if she was making a fool of me. Probably she had forgotten about when she had lived in Barlow. Luckily for her, she didn't have to look for a job like me. She always had Uncle to look after her. At this point, it occurred to me that she might not have had any problem because she had children, and she was tolerant of her husband's behaviour. In my case, it wasn't my fault that I didn't have any children. Sunil and I had decided this. Possibly, if I had had children, Sunil wouldn't have found that 'nice' Mala. I still felt bitter about it.

At the interview they asked me if I was married and whether I had children, and when I said no, they didn't want to know. I thought that they would be pleased, because I would have the chance to work extra hours if required.

I was surprised when Auntie said, 'Chit, in order to get a job, you've got to lie sometimes. By telling the truth, you won't get anywhere. So try again.'

I couldn't understand it. It seemed that the world was turning upside down. Instead of telling the truth, I was advised to lie. I was surprised at her advice because I was not used to lying. Then I thought, if I had to lie, I would lie. That was a lesson to me – in order to live and work in the city, I had to lie.

Another week went by and I was still not successful in finding a job or a place to live. Life at my aunt's home became more unbearable, especially when she said, 'If you stay here any longer, you'll have to pay for your keep.'

I was really surprised that she had come up with such a suggestion, especially when I was going through such a bad patch. I wasn't used to the idea of paying rent. I remembered how Dada from Camp Maçon didn't ask for rent when Mum went looking for a place to live, and he was a stranger to us. Mum didn't accept any rent from Uncle Sona when he stayed at our home. Above all, she was my aunt. I didn't know whether her mentioning my paying for my keep was genuine, or to make me find a job quickly.

78

'I will, Auntie,' I replied, 'as soon as I get a job.'

'Also,' she said, 'I'm concerned you'll give a bad name to the children because you left your home and husband. Besides, people will think badly of your uncle for keeping you here.'

She made me feel like a criminal, even though it wasn't my fault that I had left home. Even if I had killed myself, it would have been seen as my fault. In fact, people often believed that it was the woman's fault whenever there was a breakdown in the marriage – never the man's fault.

Because Auntie's children didn't understand life that much, I knew they had been asking her questions and that she had told them that I was staying there for few weeks, after which I would leave. When she didn't see me getting anywhere, she became anxious. I didn't have any problem with the children. They were still getting on all right with me.

When my aunt said that people would think badly of Uncle, I didn't know which people she meant. Was it the neighbours she was concerned about? I asked myself. The neighbours didn't seem to know each others' business. Or was it the relatives? She didn't specify. Besides, Uncle was hardly at home. He worked in an office and sometimes he was late coming home, by which time I was already in my room. I tried to be nice to everyone.

'I'm trying my best, Auntie.'

'I'll give you a few more weeks, and if you still haven't found a job or anywhere to stay, I'm afraid you'll have to go. I don't care where you go, but you go. I'll give you some money to last you for a while.'

I was so annoyed with her that, if I hadn't needed her help so desperately, I would have told her what to do with her money, especially when I was experiencing problems with my marriage. I was looking for love but I got scorn from my own aunt.

I didn't show my feelings to her in case she made my life more miserable. Instead, I asked her calmly, 'What will Uncle say if I stay with you for longer than expected?'

'Forget about Uncle,' she replied. 'It's me who is telling you what to do.'

I ran to my bedroom, buried my face in my pillow and cried. 'God,' I said, 'why? What have I done to be in this situation? There must be a limit to the suffering.'

Things were becoming ridiculous. She was speaking to me as if she was talking to a child. It was bad enough for Sunil to ask me to leave. Then, at least I had the chance of going back to my own home and starting life all over again. I couldn't bear the thought of people laughing at me for leaving my married home just like Mum had done. I knew that people were good at laughing at others. I often wondered if they would have come to my rescue if I was being beaten up. My mother didn't get any help. Because of that, I quite liked the people in the city. They wouldn't laugh at my misfortune. They minded their own business.

Anyway, I had my pride and I didn't want to go back to my old job, my only experience, at the Antoinette sugar estate and face Sunil and his so-called 'nice' girlfriend. I might have had a fight with the girlfriend or Sunil or both of them. That would have caused more laughter. It wasn't worth it. This could have led me to commit suicide. I came to seek refuge at my aunt's home and I didn't get much help from her. Now, having lived in the city where few people knew me, I would and could do any job I could get. Nobody would know me and nobody would laugh at me and nobody would know whether I was telling the truth or a lie.

Auntie might have contacted my uncles or Sunil, but they would have blamed me for leaving the house. So women are to be blamed again. My aunt was virtually throwing me on the street. With the thought of finding anything anywhere, I went out with fresh determination. I managed to get a temporary job in a hotel to do the cleaning and washing up. I didn't have to lie. I believed my luck had turned.

I was getting on well, and then I met a man who recommended a flat to me. The rent was reasonable and the landlord didn't care who came to see me so long as I kept the place clean and tidy. In fact, he allowed me to stay there rent-free for a month. I was so elated that I moved there within days without telling my aunt where I was going. 'Why can't everyone be like him?' I often wondered.

I didn't go back to my aunt to collect my belongings because I wasn't bothered about them, and I bought new things to use. When I moved, I decided I would make a clean break from everyone at Barlow, and with Auntie. I was still looking for a job because I didn't know how temporary my present job was going to be.

One day a man approached me and said that he wanted to be friends with me. I said to myself, why not! and agreed to his offer. He spoke plainly and said that if I agreed to sleep with him, he'd give me some money. I then thought how people had used and abused me when I was decent. Probably they would respect me if I earned money this way. I thought my decision was reasonable, and continued doing the work, although on occasions I regretted starting the business. I changed my appearance – I had my hair cut shoulder-length, I started wearing mini-skirts which I wouldn't have done in Barlow, and high-heel shoes.

My story told, I wanted to be sure Jeet fully understood my situation. I said: 'I didn't have any choice, Jeet. I hoped I would be well off, to enjoy my old age better than most decent people. I was looking for love and that's how I fooled myself by thinking that I had found temporary love. No one laughed at me, and I didn't have to worry about what people said. I still remember my aunt saying that I would have to lie in order to get anywhere, and that's how I've got by so far.'

'Chit, I like you the way you are. I'm really fascinated by your story. Although I'm a Mauritian, there were lots of things I didn't know, and I got to know them today. It is well said that we learn every day. Despite these problems, you seemed to manage well.'

'Yes, Jeet,' I replied. 'You know what they say? When you're thrown in at the deep end, you automatically know how to swim. I can't swim, but I can manage.'

'You're right there,' Jeet said.

'Anyway, Jeet, I've told you everything truly and honestly as you wanted.'

'Thank you, Chit,' Jeet replied. 'Now I know that Dad was right when he said that some women are forced into this job. I quite agree with him. I'm also very pleased with your story. One thing I'm sure of is that you're not lying to me in order to get by.'

'Jeet, I won't lie to you,' I said softly with tears in my eyes.

It was half past eleven and he still didn't want anything to eat, but preferred to have another coffee before he left.

'Some people say that you can't sleep after drinking coffee,' I said.

'It doesn't make any difference to me,' Jeet replied.

When he left, I felt as if a load had lifted off my shoulders. I felt relaxed and didn't feel like doing anything for the next few days. It was just like taking a holiday from work. I felt good in myself.

I didn't see Jeet for two weeks, then out of the blue, he came and knocked at the door.

'Good afternoon, Rakhi.'

'Good afternoon, Jeet. How are you?' I asked.

'Fine, thank you. Are you free?' he asked.

'Yes I am,' I replied. 'Come in. Would you like a drink?'

'A coffee will do, please,' he said.

'I know you only like coffee. I bought some coffee in case you popped in now and then,' I replied.

'That's nice of you.'

'I've learned a few things from you, and about you,' I said.

'Oh! What's that?' he asked.

'I've learned your catchphrase "Are you free?" and that you're always polite, and that you like coffee and Marie biscuits.'

'Rakhi,' Jeet replied, 'I have to ask you if you're free because you may be busy and don't want to be disturbed. On the other hand, when you're a nurse you automatically become polite because you've got to relate to people who are ill. I know sometimes it doesn't help to be polite. People take advantage of you as they did to you, but it's one of those things.'

'You can say that again,' I interrupted.

'As for the coffee,' Jeet continued, 'you're right. I like it and you'll find that it goes well with a Marie biscuit.'

'How was your holiday? I didn't see you around,' I asked.

'What holiday? I've been on a course at Flacq General Hospital for the last two weeks.'

'That is where my sister Diya was supposed to have got married,' I said.

'I had to stay in a room in the nurses' home. It was a long fortnight and I'm glad to be back home for a rest. We were on courses from nine 'til four. It was tiring, and instead of having an early night, all the people from the course used to meet in the hospital's social club where we played all sorts of board games until nine. So, you see, even if I knew where your sister lived, I couldn't have gone to see her. We were too busy. In fact, I would've liked to look round Flacq. I've never been there. I was also thinking about your story.'

'That was nice. Now you're home, you can go and have a good rest,' I said.

'I'm going to have a rest, but I don't know if it's going to be good. I'm back to work tomorrow. You see, we work 56 hours a week and I have to work tomorrow to make up the time.'

'I feel sorry for you,' I replied. 'But you were supposed to have been on a course!'

'Yes, I know. Because I was on a course, I've got to do six hours to make up for the time. I was given the choice to work it tomorrow or Sunday. I chose tomorrow so that I can rest on Sunday, and be able to make a fresh start next week.'

Jeet left and came back to visit me after a week.

'I've got to see you. It's very important,' he said.

'What's the matter? Come in and tell me.' I made him a cup of coffee without him asking for it.

8

A Hell of a Coincidence

'Now tell me what you've got for me. I'm all ears,' I said.

'Two days ago I went to work on Ward 10 at the hospital and saw a man from the north. I looked at his case notes, and guess what?'

'What? You tell me,' I said. 'Is this man a person you knew before, or someone who knows me?' I asked, thinking that the north of Mauritius is quite a large place, and he might have met a long-lost friend. I had lived in Cassis trouble-free for so long that I had almost forgotten I was from the north.

'He's suffering from a burst chronic stomach ulcer caused by heavy drinking,' Jeet said.

I couldn't think of anyone I knew who was an alcoholic.

'I think he's got only a few days to live,' Jeet continued, 'and he needs to talk. I thought that you could help him die peacefully.'

'Who? Me? Why me? Oh no, no! I'm not even a nurse.'

'I know that,' Jeet replied.

'Besides, I don't believe people should drink so heavily. How can I help him? I don't have any experience in nursing. You're good at it. You talk to him.'

'No, Rakhi, you can do it,' Jeet insisted, which made me a bit annoyed.

I asked him, 'Come on, why are you telling me this?'

'It's because I know you and trust you,' Jeet said. 'I know you can do the job.'

'Job? Are you being paid for this?' I asked

'No!' Jeet replied. 'You see, he looked depressed and the Matron suggested that the patient needed psychotherapy, where a trained counsellor talks to the patient and tries to help him or her with their problems.'

'No, Jeet,' I answered. 'When I was depressed, I didn't get any psychotherapy from anyone. The only thing I got was scorn, and more scorn. So I won't have a part in it. I'm not a counsellor. If something went wrong, I'd be blamed for it. Come on, Jeet, why are you insisting on this?'

'Well, when I found out more about him, for instance his name, I thought I would ask you to help, and even the matron and the doctor responsible for him said that they thought it was worth a try.'

'Well! What's his name and where does he come from?' I asked.

'His name is Mr Dutt, and he's from your village. I thought you might know him and could talk to him.'

My heart gave a thump when I heard the name. The cup I was holding fell from my hand, spilling coffee everywhere.

'I'm sorry! I'm sorry!' I said.

'It's okay! Relax, Rakhi,' Jeet said, trying to make me sit down.

It was Sunil's surname. What a coincidence! I could hardly believe what I had just heard. It was like a fairy tale. I knew it was very unusual for a matron or a doctor to ask someone completely strange to the nursing profession to do a job like this. Now I could see the connection, and the reason for the request.

I wasn't sure if it was his father, or Sunil himself, who was involved – Jeet had not told me the man's first name. I was in a daze for about a minute. Then I thought, What the heck! I don't live there any more! and I asked, 'Did you find out his first name?'

'I only know his initial. It's S, and he's 36 years old.'

'It's Sunil all right. His father's name starts with a G and he doesn't have any other relatives with that initial. I didn't know he drank alcohol. I suppose because I've been away for over ten years, anything could have happened in that time to drive him to drink,' I replied.

'You're right, Rakhi. Anything could have happened since you last saw him,' Jeet agreed.

'No, Jeet. After what I've been through, I don't think I'll be able to help you. The way I feel about him, I don't want to see him again. I feel bitter.'

'I know, Rakhi,' Jeet replied. 'You know what they say? People apologize for their sins before they die, or else they believe that their soul will not be at rest when they are dead. Come on, Rakhi. I know you're not so hard-hearted as not to forgive him, that is if he's willing to apologize for his mistakes.'

'I always thought I would let him rot in hell for the way he had treated me. Are you scared that you might lose your job or that you'll be in matron's bad books?' I asked coolly.

Jeet could see that I was growing impatient. He replied, 'Come on, Rakhi. I'm not trying to upset you. It's nothing to do with being in anyone's bad books. I'm only trying to be charitable to a human being. When you're a nurse, it doesn't matter whether you're a friend or an enemy. We treat everyone as a human being. I hope you know that we all have to die one day.'

At that moment I thought of my Mum – when she was dying, with me holding her hand. This brought tears to my eyes and made me say, 'All right, I'll do it for you.'

'That's my girl. Thank you, Rakhi,' Jeet said, giving a sigh of relief. 'It's not for me. The doctor and the matron will be very pleased if it works. I won't ask you if you're free, but please get ready tomorrow at one o'clock and it'll be helpful if you try to be brave.'

'Tomorrow?' I asked anxiously.

'Yes please,' Jeet replied. 'Because we don't know how long he's going to live. So we'll leave at one, go by bus and be at the hospital before visiting time at four.'

My stomach was churning, yet I tried to have something to eat. I was ready in time. I did my hair differently and put on make-up, which I don't usually wear. I tried my best so that Sunil wouldn't recognize me, although I didn't know if they wanted him to recognize me or not. I hoped that he didn't.

We caught a small bus, which the locals called a 'Tip-Top', from the main road and it took us about 30 minutes through the outskirts of Port-Louis to get to the hospital. On the way, Jeet told me that he had already contacted the matron and told her I'd agreed to help out. So the nurses on the ward were expecting me.

The Civil General Hospital was by the main road. My first sight of it was of a large white building with a large area in the front where people parked their cars and ambulances went in and out. There were extensions to each side of the main building which, I was told, consisted of the wards and other departments of the hospital. I could see people walking about in different types of uniforms – some of them in white overcoats, and some women in different coloured dresses and with funny caps which amused me.

'The people in white coats are doctors,' Jeet explained, 'and the women wearing caps are nurses wearing different coloured uniforms to indicate if they are qualified or not qualified. Porters wear black overalls.'

As it was out of visiting hours, we had to go through a security lodge by the main waiting room to get into the hospital. Since Jeet worked there, we didn't have any problem going in before the visiting time. As this was my first visit to a hospital, I was becoming nervous and frightened because I didn't know what to expect. I felt as if I was going for treatment myself. We went into the front building, and walked along corridors from where we could see the different wards. For me, it was like walking along corridors where everything frightened me and the echo from our footsteps didn't help. Sometimes we saw people being wheeled on trolleys. They were dressed in white gowns and had drips attached to their arms. Jeet told me that they were going for operations.

All these details weren't really sinking in, because I was frightened about how the meeting with Sunil was going to turn out. I was holding on tightly to

Jeet, and he kept on telling me to take it easy. Finally, we came to Ward 10, which Jeet told me was a surgical ward. Jeet talked to the head of the ward and then took me to meet Sunil. My stomach was churning, my heart was pounding, and Jeet kept on telling me to relax. I was even more nervous when, as it wasn't visiting time, everyone looked at me.

I saw a man with drips attached to his right arm. He was thin with sunken eyes and I almost didn't recognize him. Given the condition he was in, I didn't think he recognized me either, especially with the make-up I was wearing. He was lying there as if he was feeling sorry for himself. This made me feel sorry for him.

'All right, Rakhi,' Jeet whispered. 'I'll leave you to talk to him. I'll be in the office if you need me.'

'Jeet, please stay with me,' I implored in a whisper.

'No Rakhi, I don't think you'll be comfortable if I stay here. I'll be around if you need me.'

He introduced me to Sunil before he left.

'Mr Dutt,' Jeet talked slowly and softly, 'I'm a senior charge nurse at this hospital – I met you the other day. This is Miss Dayal. She's a close friend of mine and very religious. She has come to talk to you at the request of the matron and the doctor. You don't need to talk if you don't want to, but you can talk freely to her about anything. Anything you say will be confidential.'

I couldn't help smiling because I didn't know where he got the name from for me and, besides, I didn't consider myself religious. Yet I was praying and trying to control myself by saying, 'Please God, give me courage to talk to this man.'

'I don't mind talking to her,' Sunil said in a very faint voice.

'Thank you, Mr Dutt,' Jeet said. 'Please take your time. I'll leave you with her.'

Jeet left, went into the ward office, and watched me through the glass window. One of the nurses brought me a cup of coffee at Jeet's request. I said hello to Sunil in a soft voice, hoping that he wouldn't recognize me. I felt like shouting and swearing at him, but I tried to control myself and not to show any emotion. I had to sit nearer to him because he talked so quietly. I was terribly nervous – I was squeezing my handbag so tightly that I nearly broke the perfume vials in it. I could feel my hands sweating.

'How are you today, Mr Dutt?' I asked, trying to disguise my voice and control myself.

'I'm feeling a bit better, thank you, Miss Dayal.'

'Jeet, the person who introduced you to me, said that you had problems which led you to drinking, and that you would like to talk to someone,' I started. 'I know you had an operation a few days ago and you're feeling weak at present. Do you think you can talk to me about your problems? You don't have to, or if you wish I can come back later.'

I was surprised to hear myself talking like an expert. I didn't know where these ideas were coming from, especially when I was so nervous. I thought probably I didn't want to disappoint Jeet. I was wondering why he had told the matron that I could help Sunil. I was so busy attempting to disguise my voice that I was oblivious of my surroundings and continued talking, the eagerness fighting any nervousness that I had. I didn't even know that Jeet had came to sit behind me. He didn't tell me in case I became more nervous.

'No,' Sunil said, 'I'll talk to you now. You seem to be an understanding person.'

This was a boost to my ego because I remembered Jeet telling me the same thing when he first came to see me.

'You can speak when you feel like it,' I said.

When he started talking, he turned his face away. He was probably too embarrassed to look at me until he had finished.

'You see, I was married to a nice girl. Chit was her name,' he started. 'We liked each other a lot. We made plans about our future. After a few years of marriage, I was stupid enough to get involved with another woman, who I thought I liked a lot.'

I realized he was still using the word 'like' instead of 'love'.

He continued, 'Because of this woman called Mala, Chit and I had a row and I told her to move out. I thought Mala also liked me a lot and that I could move in with her. I then realized that Mala liked me only for my money. I didn't have any, but she insisted that I gave her a lot of money for reasons she wouldn't tell me about. I liked her and, because of that, I had to give her most of my earnings. I found out later that she was seeing another man, who was visiting her when I was working. She was using my money to buy things for him.

'Then I realized that we couldn't buy love, as I was doing for her and she was doing for that man. I also realized that Chit wasn't that type of girl. She loved me and I didn't understand the value of her love at that time. When I did, it was too late.

'I had a row with Mala and she asked me to leave and never to show my face at her home again. I came back home to find that Chit wasn't there. For the first time, I cried. I tried to talk to Mum and she was not nice to me – this was understandable.

93

I fell out with Dad. Chit's uncles threatened to beat me up until they learned that Chit was at her aunt's home. Then she disappeared before I could get to her.

'My poor Chit! I didn't know where to find her. I didn't know what to do. I couldn't eat, and the only friend I had was my bottle of rum. I was drinking day and night until I ended up here. I had an operation and now I'm in this state. Is that all you wanted to know?'

When he turned his head to face me, tears were streaming down my cheeks. Then he realized he was speaking to me, Chit.

'You must be Chit?' he asked. 'You looked different after so many years, and I didn't recognize your voice.' I couldn't say a word but just nodded. Then, with tears in his eyes and after a few minutes' silence, he continued. 'Chit, where have you been? I can't believe I am seeing you on my deathbed. How are you keeping? I suppose you won't tell me anything, but I'm pleased that you're around and well.'

I struggled for words, but managed to say, 'Fine'.

'I know I've done you wrong. If such a thing is possible, could you forgive me for what I've done to you?'

It took me few minutes to compose myself. Then I talked, using my usual voice, 'Sunil, did you think I would hang around waiting for you? Did you think that I was an ornament that you would break, mend and break again?' I tried not raise my voice, especially as I was on a ward and Jeet was nearby. I continued, 'I thought of my pride and the love of our families. I was virtually thrown on the street by my own aunt. You're lucky to see me alive, and safe and sound. I've forgotten that I had a past. Since I've been

94

doing my present job, the only thing that has mattered to me was my future. Because you're ill and have been honest about yourself to me, as I've been to someone...' (I was proud as I thought of Jeet), '...I'll pray that you'll live peacefully for the rest of your life. After today's meeting, try to forget that I ever existed and put our life together down to experience or just a dream. I wish you all the best.'

I knew that perhaps I shouldn't have said all this, but at least I was speaking my mind – saying what I had wanted to say for years. He had ruined my life and I had just learned to mend it with the help of Jeet. I knew Jeet was the person I would always adore, even if nothing came of our relationship.

'I don't mind, now that I've seen you and that you've forgiven me. Now I think I'll die in peace.'

I could see Sunil was disappointed, but also relieved. I gave Sunil a kiss on his forehead and turned to see Jeet sitting behind me.

'Oh! You gave me a shock. How long have you been here?'

'I've been here from the beginning,' he replied.

'So you heard my conversation with Sunil?'

'Yes – every bit of it,' he replied, and chuckled.

'What are you laughing at?' I asked.

'I can tell you've been crying. Your mascara has run down your cheek. Go in the Ladies' and clean yourself up.'

I went and looked in the mirror, and I looked awful with the make-up running down my cheek. I came out after tidying myself.

'Let's go before the visitors start coming in,' Jeet said. We left the ward, and I hadn't realized that Sunil had been talking to me for such a long time.

It had been an hour, but it hadn't seemed like it, especially when he had been talking so slowly.

'Bastard,' I said, later on.

'I know how you feel,' Jeet replied. 'We'll have a cup of coffee in the canteen before we go home. That'll help you cool down. Visiting time is still quite a while away.'

'Whatever you say,' I agreed.

We had a cup of percolated coffee in the canteen and some home-made cake. Jeet introduced me to some of his colleagues. After a quick chat, we came out and saw visitors waiting in the waiting room. Suddenly I caught sight of my mother-in-law, Sunil's mother.

'There's Sunil's mother,' I said to Jeet. She saw me and I don't think at first it clicked with her that it was me. She had a second look and called out, 'Daughter Chit.'

I wanted to run, but Jeet urged me to stop and talk to her. He walked away, leaving me alone with her.

'How are you, daughter? Where have you been, Chit? I was so worried about you. You didn't tell me that you were leaving us. You should have talked to me. I would have tried to help you.'

'No Mum,' I said with emotion. 'No one could have helped me, with the state I was in. I had to leave.'

'People saw you and told me that you had taken the bus for Port-Louis,' she added. 'You've changed – you look just like your mother, Monee.'

She hugged me and started to cry and I said, 'I'm all right, Mum. Please don't cry. I'm fine. I have to go. My friend is waiting for me. He's in a rush.'

'Do you know that Sunil is ill, and he's in this hospital?'

'Yes, I know, Mum. Look after him. I've got to go. See you. 'Bye.'

I broke from her embrace and rushed away, with her watching me. When we were out of sight of the hospital, we found ourselves a bench and sat down.

Jeet said, 'You shouldn't have left your mother-in-law like that. She hadn't done anything wrong to you.'

'I know,' I replied. 'I told you that I wanted to break away and make a fresh start. Anyway, what did you think of my conversation with Sunil, Jeet?'

'You were great,' he answered. 'Did you notice that he still doesn't use the word "love". I think either he's obsessed with the word "like", or he doesn't know the meaning of love.'

'You see what I mean. If you hadn't heard it, you'd have thought that I was lying or making it up,' I said.

'Tell me something, Rakhi – or shall I call you Chit now?'

'Jeet, you can call me anything you like so long as you don't swear at me. What do you want to know?'

'I think I'll continue calling you Rakhi. Tell me. If you met Sunil somewhere else, and he was fit, and he had told you his story and he was honest about it, would you have gone back to him?'

'After what I've gone through, Jeet, there was no way I could have gone back to him. You heard what I said about being an ornament. That's what I call using and abusing people. Some people take things for granted until something bad happens to them and it makes them realize that they were wrong.'

I think Jeet was impressed with my conversation with Sunil because for the first time he hugged and squeezed me, saying jokingly, 'Oh, you're awful, but I like you.'

After that he said again, 'Can I ask you something?

'Yes, Jeet. What is it now?'

'Rakhi, the matron will be pleased that you managed to talk with Sunil. I think that you deserve special thanks from her. Anyway, why don't you join the hospital as a nurse?'

'Me? A nurse? You must be joking ... aren't you?' I replied.

'No, what's wrong with that?'

'Everything's wrong with it,' I said. 'For a start, I don't have any experience in nursing. You know that.'

'Yes, Rakhi. I can talk to the matron and I'm sure she'll employ you as a nursing assistant. Nursing assistants don't need to have experience. Your talk with Sunil was a bonus, and I'm sure you'll make a good nurse. At the hospital, they'll train you. You don't have to be able to read and write so long as you can look after the patients. Caring is nursing. You can make a good career for yourself with me around to help you – unless you want to continue with what you're doing. So what do you say to that?'

'What do you mean, with you around to help me?' I said. 'You could be here today and gone tomorrow.'

'Oh, I don't know about that.'

'I don't know, Jeet. I'll have to think about it,' I replied. 'I told you that I was forced to do what I'm doing. I'll let you know later.'

'We'd better have something to eat before we go home,' Jeet suggested.

'I'm sorry, Jeet, I've not brought enough money with me.'

'Who asked you about money?' Jeet replied. 'I'll pay for the meal.'

'I'd like to share the expenses. You pay and I'll give you some money when we get home,' I said.

'Don't even think about it,' he was quick to reply.

'Whatever you say. You're the boss.'

'No I'm not. We're both the boss,' Jeet said.

We went and had a nice meal in a nearby restaurant and a nice cool glass of Mauritian Phoenix beer – the best I've had for years. We went home. Jeet went his way and I went mine. I was thinking what a day I'd had. It was such a mixture of events.

9

Good Grief – Lover's Lane Revisited

I didn't see Jeet for a week. When he came to see me, he used the same rituals – 'Are you free?' and 'I'll have a cup of coffee.' As a matter of fact, I had just finished cleaning the rooms and I was resting, hoping that I would have a peaceful afternoon.

'Yes, Jeet. Come in.'

'I came here before you have your visitors,' he said.

'Visitors? What visitors? I'm not expecting anyone,' I exclaimed.

'I thought you were. Ah well. Never mind, then. By the way, the matron gave me a letter to pass on to you.'

'That's nice of her. Please read it to me.'

Jeet read me the letter, which said that it was nice of me to go and talk to Sunil. She appreciated it very much. She also mentioned that she had a report that after I talked to Sunil, he appeared cheerful. She wanted to meet me, and would like to help me wherever she could.

After reading the letter, Jeet said, 'I've got two pieces of news for you.'

'News? Is it good or bad?'

'It all depends which way you take it,' Jeet replied.

'The first news is that the other day I was working on ward 8 when I heard that your Sunil had died. I'm sorry about that. The ritual is that the nurses bathe the body and a porter takes it to the mortuary. Relatives are informed and they take the body home to do their burial or cremation. I think your Sunil's parents were informed, and they took the body away. I didn't think you would have had the chance to go to see the body or to the funeral.'

I was affected a bit by this news. Then I realized that it was just one of those things, and tried to compose myself.

'Jeet, I respect people when they are dead. Sunil was mine until he rejected me. So I wouldn't have gone to see his body or to his funeral. I might grieve for a while, but I think it's good that he's gone because he was in such a state. I hate to see people suffer. I try my best to help wherever I can, but in the case of Sunil, the only help I could offer him was to pray for him.'

'I'm glad you think that way.'

'Now that's settled, what's your other news?' I asked.

'Oh yes,' Jeet said. 'I talked to the matron. She was pleased with your meeting with Sunil as you can see from the letter. Then I spoke to her about you joining the nursing profession. I gave her a brief rundown on you. She's willing to talk to you next Tuesday at eleven o'clock. It'll give them enough time to get your uniform and other things ready for you to start work in a fortnight. They pay you monthly by cheque, but they'll give you some money in advance so that you can get yourself organized. Are you happy with this news?'

When Jeet was telling me about the nursing job,

101

I could hardly believe this was all happening. I seemed to have gone into a dream world.

I think Jeet realized this, because he said, 'I don't think it's sinking in. I'll remind you of this later.'

I didn't know what to say to Jeet, but I replied, 'Jeet, I can't say that I'm unhappy or elated about it. I've told you that I don't have any experience in nursing. You made me believe that I could do the job because of my conversation with Sunil the other day. I think you're the judge, and you know that the job is right for me. I think I'll give it a try because you know what's best.'

'I think I'll love you for...' He didn't finish his sentence. There was a knock at the door. It was Jeet's parents. 'I think they are your visitors,' Jeet whispered to me.

'You should have told me,' I whispered back to Jeet. 'Come in and take a seat. Jeet is...' I was saying when his mother said to Jeet, 'I thought you'd be here.'

I didn't know what to do, or what to say to them, about Jeet being there. I felt a bit uneasy. 'Jeet came to tell me something when you arrived. Would you like a drink?' I asked his parents.

'A coffee will do for us. You see Jeet has got us hooked on coffee.'

I nearly said that he had got me hooked on coffee as well, but remained quiet. I brought a cup of coffee for each of us and some Marie biscuits.

When we were drinking, Jeet's mother started the conversation. I believe that women always do the talking when sensitive topics are broached. Before, I had thought that women always did the dirty work for men, but I later realized that most people like the so-called 'feminine touch', a touch of softness as opposed to men's abruptness and lack of softness.

'We're sorry to come round without warning you,' Jeet's mother said. 'We think,' she went on, 'that Jeet has been naughty for troubling you. We're sorry about it.'

'No, Auntie, you're welcome any time here. Jeet's no problem. I think he likes talking to me.'

'How are you, Chit?' she continued. I was quite surprised that she called me Chit. I realized Jeet must have told them my real name.

'I'm fine th-th-thank you.' I stuttered all of a sudden, and I could see Jeet was chuckling.

'We see you're nervous but you shouldn't be. Jeet has told us all about you.'

'Nothing bad, I hope,' I replied. I looked at Jeet. He wouldn't say anything. He was like a sheep, cornered by the presence of his parents. Unless it was that he wanted them to do the talking.

'No, girl,' his father interrupted. 'It's all good.'

'You see, Daughter,' Jeet's mother continued, 'we are very liberal. We talk freely about our problems at home. We find that by discussing things, we always manage to solve our problems. Probably you know the saying, "a problem shared is a problem solved". So Jeet told us that he loves you. That's the reason why we suggested to him that he find everything out about you that he could. We thought you were honest and you know what they say? "Honesty is the best policy". So, being honest pays in the end. We were impressed by your story – it was sad but impressive. Of course, we discussed you a lot.

'Jeet was also impressed by the way you handled the situation at the hospital. That's the reason he would like you to be a nurse. You have the ability to deal with problems. You're a mature person and we're sure that you'll like it. So it's up to you to decide what you would like to do.'

This talk by Jeet's mother reminded me of Sunil's mother. I was given the opportunity to choose on both occasions, but the difference was that this time love was mentioned instead of like – and I knew it meant love.

'Yes, Auntie, Jeet told me about it and I'm thinking about it.'

'Another thing is, Chit, that Jeet is our only child. We've not spoilt him, as he knows, yet we've tried to do everything that's best for him. He's never let us down. Since he has talked to you, he believes that he loves you and that he would like you to be his *rani*. I think you've suffered enough, and it's about time for you to settle down. Do you think Jeet is the right person for you? I don't think you'll deny that you love him, but we'll let you decide.'

Jeet looked at me. After I got over my surprise at this request, I hugged his mother and cried and cried.

Then she said, 'Control yourself, Daughter. We know how you've felt about being in this situation. You've been let down, and we assure you that Jeet is not the type of person to let you down so long as you don't let him down.'

Eventually I calmed down and could hardly believe hearing myself say, 'Auntie, do you think I'm the type of person who could let Jeet down? You know, when I wanted love, I was denied it by my father who was too concerned with his addiction. My poor mother couldn't give me enough love, though she tried hard, because she was so busy making ends meet. I thought I had the love I was looking for from Sunil, but then he got involved with his Mala.

104

I went to look for love from my aunt, my father's own sister, but I was almost thrown out on the street. In desperation, I had to do what I was doing.

'I've been searching for true love all the time. All the people I met wanted me for one thing and then abandoned me. I remember mentioning this to Jeet when he talked to me the first time. In the end, I lost hope and became a hard-hearted person. But I knew I had a soft spot for Jeet when I met him. That was the reason I poured my problems out to him. I realized he was the right person to talk to. I knew that he would listen and take notice of me. I promise you that I'll do whatever you say. You're my saviours and I respect you for that. I thank you for everything you're doing for me.'

'It means that the answer to our question is yes,' Jeet's father said. 'This will please Jeet. We're also pleased by the way things are shaping up. What we'd like you to do is to stop doing what you've been doing.'

'I've not thought of it since I first spoke to Jeet. I promise that I'll never dream of doing it again,' I replied humbly, with tears in my eyes.

'That's what we wanted to hear,' his father replied. 'If you need any help, ask us any time. We'll talk more about it next time. By the way, how are you set for tomorrow? We'd like you to come for supper with us.'

'I'd like to very much.'

'That's nice,' Jeet's father said. 'We'll see you then. We've got to go now. We'll leave you two to it. Talk to you later. Bye.'

When they left, I went and hugged Jeet as if there was no end to it, and thanked him for everything.

'Don't thank me,' Jeet said. 'Thank my parents for

105

accepting you. I've got to go now, but I'll see you tomorrow. Don't be late.'

'I thank you also for making it happen and accepting me as I am. You're an angel. I hope you'll never change like Sunil did.'

'You're an angel, not me,' Jeet said. 'Sunil changed because he was, as you said yourself, never serious. He took things for granted and he would never had made a good husband. He always thought that the grass was greener on the other side. You see, Rakhi, I read somewhere that flirting, especially when you're married, is very dangerous. Probably he flirted with Mala, or Mala flirted with him. One thing led to another, and in the end Sunil was trapped and had to treat you like he did.'

'You may be right. That could have happened. Anyway, your parents sang your praises. I want to add my bit to it.'

'Chit, I am what I am. I've always been like this and I hope that I'll stay like this. As you know I'm working an early shift tomorrow, I'll have an early night. So see you tomorrow. Don't be late. Come at about six or earlier. Please, Chit, as I've said before, try to be yourself. We live a simple life.'

'I won't be late,' I said.

When Jeet left, I watched him walk round to his home. I felt like calling him back, but I let him go. The talk about flirting confused me a bit, but I realised that harm could be done by it. I didn't know whether to cry or be happy with the thought that Jeet and his parents had accepted me as I was. In fact, I couldn't believe that was happening to me. I usually did a bit of housework and sewing in the morning, but today I couldn't set my mind to it. My heart was beating fast with excitement.

In the end, I ran to my bed and threw myself on it face down and started to cry and said, 'I thank you, God, for answering my prayer. God, why did you let me suffer that much? God, help me strengthen this relationship because Jeet is such a nice person and so are his parents. Thank you, God.'

I stayed there, and eventually must have gone into a deep sleep. When I woke up I felt relieved, as if all my anxieties and problems had evaporated. The sun was high in the sky and I felt completely relaxed. I hadn't felt like this for a very long time. Then for a minute I thought I had overslept and missed supper at Jeet's. I panicked a bit until I realized that it was only ten in the morning.

The evening came and I got ready in a casual dress and went round to Jeet's home. I went a bit early so that they wouldn't feel I was there for the meal only. Dinner wasn't ready, so I offered to help them although they urged me not to. Everyone was busy in the kitchen – Jeet's mother was baking *roti* bread and his father was helping her; Jeet was busy laying the table.

Jeet's mother said, 'You see, Chit, we were all suggesting a menu for you. Jeet was saying one thing, his father was saying another thing, and I suggested something different. In the end we've prepared a mixture of everything for you. We hope you'll like it.'

They had prepared so much food, thinking that I would eat a lot, and they wanted to please me. I replied that I didn't mind what they had cooked and that they needn't have worried to cook so much because I wasn't a big eater. The food looked delicious.

Jeet joked, 'It looks delicious and I hope it tastes delicious.'

While they were busy, Jeet's mother asked me if I could bake cakes. 'Yes I can, Auntie. I'll make some and bring them in for you.'

'We would like you to make them here so that I can learn from you,' Jeet's mother replied. 'I never had the chance to learn to bake cakes. Just tell us what ingredients you need and we'll get them for you.'

'If you say so.'

When supper was ready, we all sat at the table. Jeet's father served us Mauritian rum, although I tried to insist that I wouldn't drink. It was a Mauritian custom to insist that I try some. I tried some and they poured me some more, being careful at the same time not to get me drunk and incapable of enjoying the meal. In fact, I did enjoy the meal and, because we were talking about different things, I didn't realize that I was eating more than usual. I was also surprised that I stood the two drinks of rum. After the meal, I helped with washing and drying the dishes. I knew they were quite pleased with my company, and I was with theirs because since that day they never stopped inviting me for meals.

After the meal, Jeet walked me back home. To my surprise he gave me a long kiss on the way. Then he said, 'I'd like you to come for a walk with me one evening. We could go to La Saline beach. What do you say to that?'

'Jeet, that will be lovely. I'll leave you to decide which day. I'm all yours.'

'Well,' he said, 'I'm working late for a couple of days and I finish at one on Friday. What about Friday?'

'I don't mind. As I said, I'm all yours.'

'I'll meet you after supper at six and we can go for a stroll. I'm sure Mum and Dad will let us.'

'Jeet, I'm glad for you. You're grown up, but you still respect your parents,' I said.

'Yes, Chit,' he replied, 'although I'm grown up, I'm still their child. I don't go anywhere without telling them. They respect me for that. That's all I need – their respect and their blessing in anything I do. Anyway, it seems that it's all settled for Friday. See you then. 'Bye.'

Friday came and I got ready by five-thirty. I became anxious. I kept on looking at the time and pacing up and down the room. The time seemed to be dragging and every minute seemed to be like an hour. I was also wondering whether or not Jeet would turn up. Finally, when Jeet emerged from his house, I gave a sigh of relief. When he saw me I felt like asking him why he was late, until I realized that he was on time and it was just that I was anxious to be with him. I still said to him that he could have come earlier, to which he replied, 'I was thinking about coming earlier, but I didn't think you would be ready.'

'I was ready at 5.30, Jeet.'

'Now I know,' he said.

We hugged each other and went for a stroll along the beach with his arm round my waist and mine across his shoulders. It wasn't common for couples to walk about like that, but we didn't care what people might say.

We found ourselves a bench by the shore and sat down. The sun was just setting and the sky was glowing with its yellow rays. As La Saline was in the west, we could see the sun setting like a big yellow ball into the sea. The day's heat was lingering on

109

the land and a light cool breeze was blowing along the shore, making it a blissful evening. Behind us in the park we could hear hundreds of birds airing their evensong, adding joy to the day's end.

Jeet kissed me and asked, 'How peaceful! Are you glad you chose me?'

'Are you glad you chose me?' I asked in return.

'I think we were chosen for each other,' he said. 'It was God's doing. That's the reason we fell in love from the first time we set eyes on each other.'

'I believe in God, and this is what happened in return,' I agreed with him.

'You know, Rakhi, your love with Sunil was what I call a forced love. You didn't fall in love with him as you did with me. You learned to love each other. You tried to love him as he did you. It was false, a pretence. This is what usually happen in arranged marriages. Some people stick together for the sake of their families; not their pride but the family's pride. You were lucky that he asked you to leave, or else you'd have been sharing him.'

'We used to go out and talk about ourselves,' I interrupted.

'Yes, Chit,' Jeet said, 'but life isn't only talk. It includes deeds as well. You went to the cinema and to parks, and never took your love seriously. Even when you went out, you had chaperones and so you couldn't discuss things in private. I don't blame you for that. I understand that you needed a chaperone in case you got up to mischief. It's the custom, but I hope that one day people will learn, and make use of love marriages. Even if you'd have gone on your own, you wouldn't have built a good relationship because of the type of man Sunil was. He was, to put it crudely, jumping from one tree to another

110

without thinking of the consequences. I can gladly call our love natural. In this you don't learn to love although you learn more about each other. Love just happened. Besides, we're both mature and understand what love and life is about.'

I found Jeet's words fascinating and let him talk without interrupting.

He continued, 'You might ask why I chose you although I knew you were doing the job you did. Something else I ought to mention to you, Rakhi. One flower may blossom in a park and another may blossom in a pit of dirt, but a flower remains a flower. When you cut both flowers and put them in a vase, people will adore them. They will enjoy the scent. The beauty of the flower is you, and the scent, I believe, is your personality, your honesty and your trust. I adore you because you have all these qualities. That's the reason I told you in the beginning that you weren't cut out for the job you were doing.'

I couldn't help feeling emotional. I said, 'Jeet, I never knew that I would meet such an adorable man as you. You're understanding, a quality most people lack. I think you've waited for the right moment for your *rani* to come along.

'You know, Jeet,' I continued, 'my life has been like a jigsaw puzzle. Ever since my childhood I've been searching for the right piece to fit in. I searched for love first from my father, then from my mother and, finally, from Sunil. Now I feel I've found it, I'll keep it very close to me.'

'This is where the job comes in, Chit,' Jeet interrupted. 'By doing nursing 56 hours a week, we'll have enough time to build a life. Then we'll feel that we've achieved something. As things are at present, I don't know whether we're coming or going.'

111

'Tell me something, Jeet,' I asked. 'How come you liked me in the first place?'

'Ah! Ah! You've to be careful between like and love now. I don't know, Rakhi. When I saw you the first time, I felt something I couldn't describe. Then I said to myself, she's the right person for me. So I decided to work on it with the help of my parents. How about you?'

'I felt the same way about you,' I replied, 'but I had to leave it to fate.'

'It's getting late now. I think we'd better get back,' Jeet said.

Eight o'clock was considered late. The moon was shining and it was nice and cool, giving us a pleasant walk back home.

On the way, I said to Jeet, 'I saw so many beautiful nurses at the hospital. Why didn't you choose one of them to be your partner?'

'Chit,' Jeet replied, 'love isn't chosen. You can't choose love and say it's true love. Love can't be bought in a market. Love just happens. Our love, I hope, is true because it just happened.'

On the way, Jeet gave me some money. I didn't want to take it but he insisted, I had to buy myself some food although it was becoming a routine to have meals at Jeet's.

'I don't know how I'll repay you,' I said.

'You don't have to, but once you get your job you can help out if you want to.'

'I will, darling.'

I was surprised I had said 'darling'. The word became natural in our conversation later on. It made me feel closer to Jeet than I was with Sunil. When Jeet was saying goodbye on my doorstep, something happened when I least expected it. He looked into my eyes and I looked into his, and we were drawn irresistibly closer and closer. We embraced, and we kissed and kissed. We hugged each other as if the moment would never end. We stayed like that for at least five minutes.

'You know, Chit,' he whispered, 'I've found what I've been waiting for. You're the one for me. I knew it as soon as I set eyes on you. I've never loved anyone and I've never felt like this before. Don't you ever fail me.'

'Jeet,' I whispered back, 'I'll never fail you. This is the moment I've been waiting for as well. I love you. I love you with all my heart, Jeet.'

'I love you,' Jeet replied, 'and I'll never let you down.' We kissed again. 'I wish we didn't have to go our separate ways, but I'm sure it won't be long,' he reassured me. We didn't want to part yet we did, reluctantly.

I felt as if I was in a different world. I hadn't felt like this when I was with Sunil because, as Jeet had said, it had been a forced love. Now I promised myself that from now on, I would never make comparisons between my relationships with Sunil and with Jeet. Before he left, Jeet reminded me not to forget my interview the following week.

'You've to take me there, anyway,' I said.

'Yes, darling. I will. I've taken a day off just for that. So please don't let me down.'

10

My New Job

After the meeting on Friday, I felt I wanted to be in the Jeet's company for longer at a time. Time didn't allow us because he was working, but also we didn't want to rush things.

On Monday, Jeet was doing a late shift at work. When he came home at 8.30 in the evening, he came round to inform me that we would leave at 10.00 in the morning. He couldn't stay for coffee because he said he was tired and wanted to have an early night.

I couldn't sleep properly that night. I tossed and turned, excited at the prospect of a new job. I knew that it would be different from my work in the sugar cane field – if I got the job. It would be a new challenge. At least I would be working with people, 'understanding and caring for them' as Jeet used to say.

I got up early in the morning with my eyes still burning from my restless night. As the time approached, I became increasingly nervous. I tried on about five dresses trying to decide which one would be best for the interview. I finally chose one, but I was still not sure if it was appropriate. I was ready by 8.30 a.m. I became so nervous that I couldn't sit still. One minute I was pacing up and down the lounge, the next I was sitting and fidgeting my fingers or looking at myself in the full-length mirror, adjusting my dress and checking I was presentable. I had been to the toilet about three times. I was so nervous that I couldn't eat or drink anything. I was particularly nervous because I had heard that matrons were usually very strict with nurses although I realized that they could also get on well with the nurses. It seemed that Jeet got on well with the matron. I tried really hard to calm myself, but it was impossible. I felt relieved when Jeet came in at 9.30.

'Oh, you look radiant in your blue dress,' he exclaimed. 'Blue is my favourite colour.' He then said, 'Relax, Chit, you're only going to see the matron. She doesn't know you but she knows of you. She's friendly and you'll like her.' I felt a bit more relaxed then.

We caught the bus and we were at the hospital by 10.30. I had time to relax myself over a cup of coffee, but the thought of meeting the matron was still at the front of my mind. At eleven o'clock we went to see the matron in her office. The matron was stern-looking, but pleasant to talk to. She welcomed us and made us feel relaxed by offering us a drink.

After five minutes of talking about the hospital to Jeet, she turned to me and said, 'Sorry, I didn't mean to ignore you, but we had to sort out a few things. My name is Miss Conhye. So you're the person with talent who helped us by talking to Mr Dutt. You see, Mr Dutt needed someone to talk to and after you had been to see him, he cheered up a bit. He looked quite content in himself. In the end, he died peacefully. We thank you very much for your help. We wrote to you and, because we

115

didn't have your address, we sent the letter with Mr Dayal here.'

'Many thanks, Matron, I got your letter. I'm glad I was of help to you. I feel that I would like to do more to help people wherever and whenever I can.'

I was surprised to find I was talking with such enthusiasm despite being so nervous. This made me realize that I could do anything if I put my mind to it.

'That's nice,' the matron said. 'That's the spirit! Thank you again. Mr Dayal told me that you want to join the nursing profession although you don't have any experience. We need people with an interest like yours. You see, most of our nurses don't have any experience when we recruit them, so you don't have to worry about that, because we train you on the ward.

'Mr Dayal also said that you don't have any qualifications. We usually recruit people with School Certificate for this job, but since we know you and you're Mr Dayal's fiancée, we'll take you. The rest is up to you. Just give me your full name and date of birth and leave the rest to me.'

'My name is Chitrekha Roop. They call me Chit for short.'

Matron filled in a form and said, 'Mr Dayal will take you to the hospital's general store and tell the people to have a suitable uniform ready for you. We would like you to start on Monday. You have one week to prepare yourself. Can you start on Monday?'

'Yes, Miss Conhye. Thank you for your help.'

'You're welcome, Miss Roop. See you next week.' She turned to Jeet and said, 'Your fiancée is beautiful. You've got good taste.'

'Thank you, Matron.'

116

When we came out, I was so overjoyed at getting the job that I hugged and kissed Jeet, and thanked him for his help. I was also thinking that it was not a case of what one knew, but who one knew.

Then I said to Jeet, 'Do you go round telling people that I'm your fiancée?'

'How else do you want me to introduce you to my friends? I think that's the only way, darling.'

Then I said, 'I didn't know your name was Dayal.'

'Well,' he replied. 'You never asked me. I didn't know your name was Roop.'

'Well,' I replied, 'you never...'

'I know. I never asked you.'

We went to the general store. I tried on some uniforms and managed to get some to fit. I left them at the store to be collected on the day I started work at the hospital. During the week, I got a letter from the matron through Jeet stating that I was to report to Ward 3 the following Monday at nine o'clock. It was a medical ward.

On Monday, I was nervous again because I didn't know what to expect. Jeet told me Ward 3 was a female ward for patients with different illnesses. He said he knew the charge nurse and that she would tell me what to do. The work on the ward would give me the chance to get to know something about diseases and the symptoms people suffer.

Jeet accompanied me the first day. By this time I was used to the bus system and knew where to get on and off. This meant that Jeet wouldn't have to go with me all the time, except when we were both on the same shift. He reminded me, 'I trust you to travel on your own.'

'Yes, darling,' I replied. 'You can trust me. I'll be all right. Don't worry about anything.'

117

I picked up my uniform and we both went to the ward where we were greeted by the charge nurse, a nice young girl in a blue uniform. I put on my uniform and Jeet gave me a wolf-whistle. He whispered to me that I looked great in the uniform, although I didn't feel comfortable, especially with the cap on. But when I saw other nurses wearing similar caps, I didn't feel so embarrassed. Jeet left and said he would pick me up at five when my shift ended.

'I'm Sister Rose. You can call me Sonya. Welcome to Ward 3, Miss Roop – or shall I call you Chit?' the sister said.

'Please call me Chit.'

'Come to the office and we'll talk about the work,' the sister continued and we went in. 'Jeet told me that you don't have any experience in nursing. Don't worry. You'll soon get the hang of it. Before we do anything, take this key and put your stuff in that locker over there. Keep the key with you and don't lose it.'

I put my belongings in the locker and went back to the office. 'Right,' the sister said, 'I'll tell you what we usually do when we come on duty. First of all we tick ourselves off on this register, and then we have a report on the patients, and either I or my deputy allocate who looks after which patients. We have an hour's lunch break. When we finish our shift, we tick ourselves off again. You don't have to do much this week. Work alongside Nurse Meena. She's quite good and she'll explain to you what goes on. Good luck.'

'Thank you, Sister. I need it.'

She called Nurse Meena and introduced me to her, and to four other nurses who worked on Ward 3.

Nurse Meena showed me around. On the way we talked to some patients. Some of the patients were too ill to move and others had drips attached to their arms. This sight brought tears to my eyes because I thought of my mother. I didn't show my emotion. I got on well with the nurse and she explained about the patients' care.

She also mentioned, 'When I first started, I was very emotional, especially when someone died. I got counselling from the sister until I became tougher, although I can still become emotional.'

'That's natural, I think,' I replied. 'I'll try my best to contain myself when that sort of situation arises.'

'I was told that you're Mr Dayal's fiancée. Where are you from? Sorry, what's your name again?'

'Yes, I'm his fiancée, and they call me Chit.'

'That's a nice name.'

The day was not as bad as I had expected and, certainly, the sister and other nurses were helpful. We were quite busy and I was surprised when it was time to go home. It was five o'clock and Jeet was waiting for me outside.

'You may go,' the sister said. 'You were good and helpful. I think we'll like your company.'

'Thank you, Sister,' I replied.

When I came out after changing into my own clothes and locking the uniform away in my locker, Jeet kissed me and asked how my first day had been as a nurse.

'Oh, great!' I replied. 'I think I'm going to like it. I didn't know that nursing was so interesting. I'd like to thank you for everything you're doing for me.'

'Don't mention it,' he replied. 'I'm glad you like it.'

'I like it very much. What I need now is to go straight home and have a good bath before I do anything else,' I said to him.

I was asked to carry on with the same routine for the whole week. Then I was given shift work. I didn't mind that, except that when I had to work in the morning, I had to get up very early to be able to start work at seven o'clock. This reminded me of the time when I used to work on the sugar estate and woke up at five. The only difference was that I was now used to getting up late and I was finding it hard to get up early. A few weeks went by without any incident. I got on well with everyone. I learnt a lot. I learned to face the sights of cuts and bruises. Whereas before I had dreaded the sight of blood, after working on the ward I was getting used to it. Sometimes I worked on different wards, and I didn't mind working on any of them. In fact, nursing offered me more than I had expected. I was grateful to Jeet who had enticed me into this profession.

11

Happy Ever After

Jeet was proud of me and so were his parents. One Sunday both Jeet and I were off duty when Jeet said, 'Mum and Dad have invited you for tea at three. They would like to talk to you.'

'I'll try my best. What's it all about?' I asked.

'I don't know. Perhaps they would just like you to have tea with them.'

'We always have tea together. I'll see you then.'

On Sunday, I woke up early. I did my washing and ironing. I cleaned the flat and had a shower. I went round to Jeet's house at 2.30 p.m. and saw his mother was baking some cakes, which I had taught her how to do and given her the recipe for. His father was busy in the garden tending the flowers. When he came in, he brought some freshly cut roses which said were for me. Jeet was busy doing some paperwork. I offered to help his mother with the cake, but she said she would like to do it herself to see how she got on. I said that she was doing very well. It was nice and sunny, so we laid the table in the garden under a large parasol. It was about 3.30 when we all sat down.

We had some cake, and during coffee Jeet's mother started the conversation.

'I baked these cakes using Chit's recipe. See how you like them.'

'These aubergine cakes taste delicious and they are well cooked,' I complimented her, 'and the bhajias taste nice as well.'

'Next time I'll try the gateau piment [chilli cakes].'

After we had finished tea, she said, 'It was a nice tea. Thanks for coming to tea with us. I can honestly say that we enjoy your company. We wish that you would always stay with us. Jeet's father and I have talked to Jeet. We've also seen how much you're both in love, and we believe that you can't go wrong with this relationship and with our help. So we've decided it would be a good idea for Jeet and you to be married.'

I kept quiet and bent my head.

'We won't rush you into it,' she continued. 'We'll let you decide. We've decided that it won't be a big wedding. There'll be a ceremony at home. The registrar will come home and marry you officially. We'll let you think about it. If you decide against it, we won't hold it against you. We'll still be friends with you and you can still come and go as you do now.'

I remembered that Heera's parents hadn't given me such a choice, and I also remembered that Uncle Sona had said that his girl wasn't given the chance to choose – whereas now I was. I didn't give her a reply. We got up and I helped Jeet's mother with the washing up, and Jeet helped with drying the plates without me saying much. I left with Jeet's mother giving me some cakes to take with me.

Jeet came to see me later in the evening, which I expected. I hugged him and cried. I didn't make a cup of coffee because I was still full from the

122

afternoon tea and so was Jeet. I was in an emotional state because I was wondering whether getting married the second time was going to work out or not. I wanted reassurance that Jeet wouldn't end up like Sunil, falling prey to another girl. The only consolation I had was that I had loved Jeet from the start, and he me.

So I said to him, 'Jeet, I know you love me. You know I love you very much. It was because of you that I've come this far. I couldn't talk to your mother without talking to you about it again. I've been hurt, Ject. You know that I was driven to an immoral job. Yet, even after knowing this, you want to marry me?'

'Chit,' he replied, 'I know you've been hurt in the past. I urge you to forget the past and think what lies ahead. You remember my theory about the flower and the scent. Well, it stands. You also have to remember that this is love, and not like it was with Sunil.'

'If that's the case,' I replied with a smile, and tears in my eyes, 'I love you as always and I would like Mum and Dad to go ahead with the plan.'

'That's my girl. You got me worried for a minute in case you had changed your mind.'

'I'm sorry, Jeet,' I replied. 'I'm a woman and I desperately want your love and reassurance.'

'You have everything you want,' Jeet said. 'You're mine and I can shout it to the world. Remember always that I'll never let you down. Tell you what.'

'What?' I asked.

'It's best you tell Mum and Dad about your decision. They asked you the question. We can have a special meeting next Sunday, and you tell them then.'

'I'll do that, Jeet,' I said.

We met the following Sunday for tea and, as it

was warm and sunny, we were sitting outside having a cup of tea. Jeet's mother raised the subject again.

'Daughter, have you decided what you want to do?'

'Mum,' I said, 'you know that I've been searching for love all my life. Now that I've found what I've been looking for, I desperately want it to flourish. Since you know my life story and still want me to be your daughter-in-law, I'll accept your offer.' I looked at Jeet and continued, 'Jeet and I love each other. Together, we've made a sound foundation for a relationship which, I pray to God, will never break down.'

Jeet spoke then, and said, 'Chit, I know you've been through a lot, and I think it's about time you enjoyed yourself. I promise I'll never let you down. I know you love me and you know very well that I love you. We'll work together to make it last forever.' We talked in front of his parents as if we were swearing an affidavit in court.

Jeet's father poured some champagne, which he had brought from indoors for all of us and said, 'Chit, you've been brave. All we have to do now is to toast this happy occasion. Welcome to the family, Chit. Cheers.' Then he added, 'We've been married for fifty years. We met when we were working on the estate. We are still happy together. So I agree with Jeet that a love marriage is the best policy.'

'We'll drink a toast to that,' Jeet and I said.

'If that's settled,' Jeet's mother said, 'we'll talk to the priest and the registrar to see when they can perform the wedding. We'll allow plenty of time so that it'll give us chance to prepare properly and invite some close friends and relatives. As for your house, you'll have to decide what you want to do with it, Chit. You can talk to the landlord, explain the situation to him and return it to him. I know you've lived there for a long time, but I'm sure he'll understand. Wait until after the wedding, and then decide. As for your nursing work, if you're happy with it, you can continue doing it or, if you prefer, you may stay at home.'

'Of course,' Jeet's father intervened, 'we're not forcing you in anything. You decide what's best for you.'

I was thinking that I had stayed at home after I got married to Sunil and, in the end, I had lost everything. I didn't want this to happen again. So I said, 'I'll see how I get on, but for the time being, I think it's best to leave things as they are.'

Exactly one week after I was there for tea, Jeet's mother told me that the wedding ceremony was fixed to take place in seven weeks, at their house, giving us time to prepare and invite whoever we wanted to.

She added, 'I don't think you have anyone you'd like to invite. It's up to you. You may invite the landlord and his family. You may like to invite your people.'

'Yes, I think the landlord is the only person I know here that I can invite. I may also invite some close friends from the hospital. As for my family, I've lived away for a long time and I think I'll leave it like that.'

'I think Jeet has invited some of his friends, including the matron,' Jeet's mother said. 'I don't think the matron can come, because she has already made some other arrangements. Don't worry about preparing any clothes or food for the occasion. Think that you're our daughter and that we're getting you married at our expense. Besides, Jeet always wanted a simple wedding.'

'That's nice of you.' I hugged her and continued,

125

'You're like a mother to me. But I wouldn't like you to think that I'm not contributing anything towards the expense.'

'I'll never think that way, my dear,' Mum replied.

'Thank you very much,' I said. 'I don't know how I'll repay you.'

'You repay us by being a good daughter-in-law,' she was quick to reply.

Jeet and I had made more trips to La Saline beach and the park next to it, and also had plenty of romantic moments. Both of us booked a week's holiday from work so that we could enjoy our honeymoon together, and we were given another complimentary week by the matron. Both of us received a lot of presents from people, although they couldn't be there on the day.

We started preparing for the wedding from Saturday, and I was at Jeet's house from the morning onwards. A small tent was pitched in front of the house to accommodate the few guests, and food was prepared for them. On Sunday, a few people arrived with their presents and I was introduced to them. I was glad that my landlord had come as well. He congratulated me and said, 'I don't think you'll need your flat now. I don't mind if you decide to give it back. It was nice having you. See what you decide, and let me know.'

'Thank you for helping me when I needed it most. I really appreciated it. You helped me a lot, and I'll never forget it, or you.'

As I became emotional and hugged him, he said, 'Calm down, girl. You needed help and I helped you the best way I could. Now it's your big day and I want you to be happy. Don't worry about paying the rent. Take it as my present for your wedding.'

'Thank you! Thank you.' I hugged him again.

Dinner was served before the wedding ceremony at one o'clock. The registrar came at twelve o'clock and a wedding document was signed with two witnesses countersigning it – a procedure that hadn't occurred when I married Sunil, indicating that officially my first wedding didn't happen, and I couldn't claim anything from the family if I wanted to. The priest arrived. He had his dinner and the ceremony was started exactly at one o'clock, in the tent. The wedding wasn't as extensive as my first one had been because, as Jeet had wanted, it was just to recognize that we were married officially and in religion. After the ceremony, we met and chatted to the guests. We didn't go away to the groom's home, nor did we have to comply with a female escort for me. We were lucky that most people had left by the end of the day, leaving us to relax and prepare for our honeymoon.

On Monday morning we got up quite early, although it was our day off. Jeet asked me to pack some clothes as we were going away for the night. He didn't tell me where we were going and how long for – it was to be a wedding surprise. So we took our small suitcases and set off at about three in the afternoon.

'Where are we going, Jeet?'

'Chit,' Jeet replied, 'it's a surprise. I know you need a break from everything, and so do I.'

We took a bus to Curepipe where we changed to go to the south. We got off at 5.30 and walked a little distance, yet he still wouldn't tell me where we were going. Then we reached a guest house, with a sign outside saying 'CONGRATULATIONS TO JEET AND CHIT'. As I couldn't read, apart from names,

Jeet read the sign to me. I was so surprised that I didn't know what to say to him.

We went into the house. The landlord and landlady, with a few other people, came to greet us with a tray of glasses full of champagne. They all greeted us: 'Three cheers to the newly married couple, Jeet and Chit. Hip! Hip! Hooray! Hip! Hip! Hooray! Hip! Hip! Hooray!'

I couldn't say a word. I could feel tears flowing down my cheeks. In the end, I composed myself and thanked Jeet for such a lovely surprise. A party was held in our honour that night. People continually congratulated us and gave us drinks. We tried to restrict ourselves to only a few drinks, so that we wouldn't spoil our stay by being drunk or having a hangover the next day. We danced away until about 10 p.m., when we were really tired and went to bed. It was then that Jeet revealed we were staying there for the week.

'Why didn't you tell me, Jeet? I could have brought more clothes and towels.'

'Don't worry, Chit. That's another surprise. Mum packed some extra clothes, towels, and bathing costumes for you in my case. My clothes are also in the bag I've brought.'

'Do you like giving surprises, darling?' I asked.

'On occasions like these – yes!' Jeet replied.

'I wonder what other surprises you've got in store for me!'

'You have to wait and see, Chit.'

'By the way, Jeet,' I asked, 'how did you come to book this place for our honeymoon?'

'I came here a few weeks ago with a friend, and made all the arrangements to surprise you.'

'To be honest, Jeet, I'm really amazed at what you've done to please me. Thank you.'

We spent most of the week travelling by bus. The first day we didn't go that far, yet we took a couple of towels and our bathing suits – just in case we needed them, Jeet said. The landlady prepared a packed lunch in case we didn't find a shop to buy food on the way. We went to a seaside resort which Jeet said was called Gris-Gris, and which was only about a mile from the hotel.

'Wow! How beautiful!' I exclaimed.

'It is, isn't it?' Jeet said. 'I've never been here before.'

We stood on top of the cliff, from where we could see a stretch of white sandy beach down below, and the calm sea. A cool breeze was blowing and, although it was a hot September day, we didn't feel the heat.

I was so keen to get myself into the water that I begged, 'Please, please, Jeet, let's go down. How do we go down?'

To get there, we had to follow a lane with purposely built rocky steps. I couldn't wait to get there and paddle in the water. There weren't too many people around because it was a weekday, and so we had the beach to ourselves. As soon as we were there, I pulled Jeet along, running, splashing and kicking up the water. We dug into the sand trying to see who would find water first.

Later we put on our swimming costumes and went to play in the water. I couldn't swim but I was surprised to see Jeet swimming well. After this, we spread out our towels and lay down, enjoying the cool breeze from the sea. The ripples on the beach were a lullaby to my ears, and I dozed off in no time. I woke up completely relaxed, and we had our lunch. With the excitement, we forgot that it was nearing four o'clock. We left fully relaxed.

'What a beautiful day we've had, Jeet!' I hugged him and gave him a lingering kiss. 'It's all thanks to you!'

After such a lovely experience, we went to look around the southern village of Souillac (pronounced Sooyaak) and went back to the hotel after an exhausting day.

I was wondering what other surprises Jeet had in store for me. I asked him, but he said that I had to wait and see. The following day he told me to get ready as we were going to a place as exciting as the previous day. We took a packed lunch and our swimsuits as well as our towels. We took a bus from Souillac and, after a 30-minute ride, we reached a place which Jeet said was called Blue Bay.

I looked at it and exclaimed, 'Wow! How beautiful! They have such beautiful places in the south. It's wonderful.'

'Yes, it is. I've never been here before either.'

Blue Bay was the most beautiful spot I had ever visited. The sky was blue and it gave a deep blue reflection to the sea. The white sandy beach stretched for miles. Jeet and I walked and walked, and didn't feel exhausted. We put on our bathing costumes and went into the water, which was nice and warm. Because it was low tide, we walked into the sea for about half a mile. We played in the water for quite a while.

Later, we sat down under the filao trees and enjoyed the cool breeze from the sea. I felt ecstatic, with the cool breeze and having Jeet next to me. It was bliss. We enjoyed every minute of it. We had our packed lunch, although we weren't feeling hungry.

We didn't want to leave, but we had to because we had to catch the bus back. We wanted to go back to Blue Bay, but we since heard about other lovely resorts nearer home, such as Flic-en-Flac in the west and Grand Bay in the north.

One day during the week, Jeet hired a taxi for a long-distance trip. He wouldn't tell me where to. The taxi kept on going, along a winding road and towards a hilly place inland.

'It isn't the seaside, because we've left the sea behind?' I asked.

'Wait and see, Chit.'

The only things I could were wooded areas on both sides until we arrived at a special place.

'This is Chamarel, a place noted for its seven-coloured earth,' Jeet said.

'Jeet, you certainly know how to surprise me, don't you?' I said softly.

'I'll do anything to make you happy, Chit.'

'Thank you, Jeet. Thank you.'

That trip was also fantastic, because we had the chance to walk on mounds of different coloured natural soil in the middle of nowhere.

'They say that no matter how much soil they remove from here,' the taxi driver said, 'the mounds do not seem to go down. It's a mysterious place.'

We both enjoyed it for its uniqueness and mystery. We collected some soil and left. On the way back, we stopped and picked some guyaves de Chine (yellow guyavas) which we enjoyed eating.

Above all, we had a great time in the south. We intended to go there again later. For now, we had to return home.

On the way back, I was content, and I asked, 'Tell me, Jeet. How did you know where to go to and how to get there?'

'When I came to make arrangements for the

honeymoon, I asked the hotel keeper for all the information. He told me where to go and how to get there. He also suggested the surprise welcome at the hotel. I thought it was a good idea and went along with it.'

'It was all to please me!'

'All to please you, Chit. You deserved it.'

'Thank you, Jeet. Thank you.'

We used the second holiday week visiting friends and Jeet's relatives, because we knew that once we started work, we wouldn't have much time to visit people. It was during this week that I gave my flat back to the landlord, although he said he felt sorry that I was leaving. Jeet and I continued to work at the hospital. We seemed to be growing fonder of each other every day. Then we decided to start a family.

After two years of marriage we had a baby boy, who we decided to call Ajay. Jeet chose Ajay because he had an uncle by that name who had helped the family a lot when they needed it. I was glad that I had a boy, after what I had been through. 'One day I was on my own and I held the baby and said to myself, 'Mum, see you've got a grandson from your eldest daughter. Look after him so that no harm comes to him. I don't know what happened to Diya, Rena and Deep, but I hope they are fine. God, thank you for looking after me and rewarding me with a beautiful son.' While I was speaking, I noticed Jeet was in the room and then, regardless of his presence, I continued, 'God, thank you for giving me a husband who understands me and who has given me such a nice present.'

Jeet held me and kissed me and the baby.

After the first child, we decided not to have another

one. But everyone was urging us to have another child so that Ajay could have a brother or sister to call his own after we died. At first, we disregarded everybody's advice. Then we thought that perhaps people were right, that Ajay needed a brother or sister of his own or else he would feel lonely. Jeet, for instance, sometimes wished he had a brother or sister of his own. So we tried again, and after few years we had a baby girl whom we named Madhu, which means sweet. Jeet's parents were pleased when we presented them with two grandchildren, and they got on very well with them. Ajay also got on well with his little sister Madhu. We didn't spoil the children, but Mum and Dad did.

I had washed my hands of my family in Barlow. One day Ajay asked me if I had any brothers and sisters. He had asked the same question of Jeet, and he knew that Jeet didn't have any brothers or sisters. I then realized that I was wrong to give up my family. After all, they had not done anything wrong to me. So I told Ajay and Madhu the truth. Since then I had a great urge to see my brother and sisters. I even got paranoid because, whenever I saw someone going past, I was thinking they looked like my brother or sisters. I talked to Jeet about my desire and he said that we would go and see them one day.

One Sunday we decided to take a day trip to Barlow. Hoping that everyone would be at home, we took a bus and off we went. I almost didn't recognize the place where I had spent my childhood. It was over 20 years since I had been there. It had not occurred to me to go there. There were a lot of new houses. Older people I had known were either too old to be recognized, or dead. Youngsters of my time were grown up, and most of them were married and had children of their own. Four of us went to my old home, where an extension had been built in the front. The thatched roof had been replaced by a concrete flat roof. I rang the door bell and a man in his late thirties answered the door, holding a little boy by his hand.

He said, 'Yes? How can I help you?'

'Who are you?' I asked.

'That's funny. You rang the bell and asked me who am I. My name is Deep. Who are you to ask me who am I?' he replied.

'Deep. Don't you recognize me?'

'No, I don't,' he said harshly.

'Deep, look at me and see if you don't recognize me.' He was about to slam the door on me when I said, 'Deep. Don't you recognize your own sister, Chit?'

He froze where he was standing, and could not say a word. Then he said, 'Chit? You mean, my Chit?'

'Yes, Deep, your Chit.'

Then he hugged me tight and cried like a baby. He said, 'Sorry, but it has been so long. How are you, Sister? Where have you been? Why didn't you come to see us? Why? Why, Sister?'

He was asking me all these questions, expecting me to answer them all at once. I felt like asking him a hundred questions all at one once, but I said, 'Deep. Calm down. I've come to see you and I shall tell you all about what has happened. But first, let me tell you that this is my husband and this is our son, Ajay, and daughter, Madhu. Can we come in now?'

He greeted everyone and said, 'Yes, Sister. This is your house as much as it is mine. Come in. Come in.'

'How are you...?'

While I was asking him this, a young woman walked

in. 'This is Ooma, my wife. Ooma, this is my sister, Chit, I was always telling you about. We got married six years ago and we've a son, Ash, who is five.'

'Where's Uncle Sona?' I asked.

'He's in his room. I think he's got flu and is running a temperature.'

'Let's go and surprise him,' I said.

Instead of sitting down, we all went straight into his room. I think he was just dozing off. I sat on his bed.

'I told you not to wake me up,' he called out. He looked up and then away again. He looked a second time, and sat straight up.

'Chit!' he exclaimed. 'Are you real or am I dreaming?'

He got up and hugged me, and was surprised to see so many people in his room. I introduced Jeet, Ajay and Madhu to him.

'Tell me, Chit. Where have you been? Why didn't you come here before you left for Ste Croix. My sister Savi wasn't nice to you, but she said she would apologize to you when she saw you. But after not seeing you for so many years, we thought we'd never see you again.'

'I'm fine, Uncle. I'm sorry I had to leave without seeing you, but Sunil was rotten to me,' I said.

'I know,' Uncle Sona said. 'He came and apologized for his bad behaviour. He lost everything, didn't he? He took to drink, and I was told that he died in hospital from a burst stomach ulcer.'

'I know, Uncle,' I interrupted. 'I went to see him.'

'You went to see him?' he asked. 'How did you know about it?'

'Well,' I said, 'Jeet is a nurse there and he told me. I didn't want to know at first, but Jeet urged me to go and see him.'

135

Deep was sitting with his son Arun on one of his knees and Madhu on the other. Deep had changed and grown up. Uncle Sona had aged a bit, and he said that I had put on weight. He recognized me straight away, because I was the spitting image of my mother. Deep hadn't recognized me because he was still very young when Mum died.

'What are you doing these days?' I asked Deep.

'I have to thank Uncle here for encouraging me to continue with my studies. I am grateful to him. I got through my exams, went for my teacher training and now I'm working at Amaury's Primary School, working in year five. I like my work and I look forward to it.'

The name Amaury made my anger rise, because that was where Heera's Mala lived, but I didn't show this to anyone. I realized that had been a blessing in disguise, and I was happier with a good man like Jeet.

While we were talking away, Deep's wife had prepared a meal, and now she called us to the table. It seemed that Uncle Sona's flu had gone with the excitement, although he still had a light cough.

'How are Diya and Rena, and how are the other uncles?' I asked.

'Diya didn't get married to the man from Flacq,' Uncle Sona replied, 'because he decided to go abroad to study. So Diya got married to a policeman in Grand Bay. The beach is only twenty minutes' walk from where she lives. She's got two sons, Anoop and Raj. Every time we go there, we go for a picnic under the filao trees. The beach is beautifully white. You must go there some time.'

'Sometimes we stay late,' Deep added, 'and go to catch crabs by torch light. It's fun.'

'Yes. One bit Daddy's fingers with its legs,' Ash said.

'By legs, Ash means pincers,' Deep explained.

'Anyway,' Uncle Sona continued, 'Rena is married to a man in Rose-Hill. She was married in the south, but they moved there. Her husband is a builder. They also have two sons, Sar and Sunny. She has bought a little confectionery shop close to a bus depot, where she sells sweets, cigarettes, and also home-made cakes. Rena is always busy and we hardly see her, but Diya comes to see us quite often. As for my two brothers and sisters-in-law, they are all fine. They are getting on a bit, but they are fine. We often talk about you. You should meet them.'

'We can't do it today. If you like, you can organize a family reunion on a Sunday,' I suggested.

'That's a good idea. Will the fourth Sunday be okay? It'll give people the chance to get time off from whatever they are doing and come along.'

'I think Jeet can get time off as well,' I said.

'What a coincidence!' Jeet replied. 'I'm on holiday that week. Yes, we can make it.'

Uncle Sona said, 'Leave it to me to organize that. You know something? Chit is the centre of attention and yet we were so excited that we forgot to ask her how she's been.'

'It shows how you care for me,' I said. 'Yes, after I left Auntie Savi, I rented a flat and worked part-time in a hotel. I left the job to do something else until I met Jeet. I worked as a nurse full-time at first and now I do part-time because of the children. Mum looks after the children when I'm at work. Of course, Ajay goes to college now and Madhu will start school next year. She's five now. Otherwise, I'm fine. I can't complain.'

137

After the meal, I sat and talked. I didn't go to see the village, because I thought I'd leave it for next time, although I wanted to see how it had changed. But Jeet and the children went to look around Barlow. They liked it, because Jeet said it reminded him of where he used to live, Trianon. We had a cup of tea and we left at four because it was getting late. The children weren't used to travelling long distances and had to be in bed early in order to be fresh for school on Monday.

'We hope to see everyone on the fourth Sunday,' I said as we left. Jeet and the children were pleased they had seen my family.

The days went by slowly, probably because I was so eager to meet my sisters and their families, and my uncles and aunts.

The day came. I asked Jeet's mother and father if they would come along. Dad was getting on a bit and couldn't travel long distances, but Mum decided to come. We went there by bus because we didn't have a car, although we were planning to buy one. If Dad had come, we could have hired a car. Considering that bus services to Barlow were still a problem, as I had known before, we were there by eleven o'clock.

I was so surprised and excited to see all the guests that had come. I was busy meeting my sisters and their families, and the uncles with their families. There was emotion all round. They'd all changed over the 20 years. The uncles had gone grey. Diya had grown slim and tall. I wasn't sure who she took after. I believed it could have been someone on my mother's side. Rena took after my father, and so did Deep. There were two people I least wanted to meet: Sunil's mother and Auntie Savi. I asked Uncle Sona why he had invited them.

He replied, 'Chit, I know you've been through a lot. You've got to understand that Sunil's mother hasn't done anything wrong. In fact, she tried to help you a lot. Since you left, she has lost her only son, and her husband. So you can't just reject her. Now look at my sister Savi. She was rotten to you, but probably she was under some sort of pressure – you know women have their problems. She has realized her mistake, and she's prepared to make it up with you.'

'Come on, Chit,' Jeet interrupted. 'You said you believe in God. You forgave Sunil. You can forgive an ageing person like your aunt. You know the well known saying, "God forgives those who forgive themselves." I have learned it as school and I believe in it. After all, I'm sure today is a great day for you.'

'I suppose you're right, Jeet.'

As I was saying this, Auntie Savi came to me and said, 'I suppose you won't talk to me, Chit. I know that because of me, we lost you for more than twenty years.'

'Auntie,' I replied, 'you did what was best for you.' I couldn't control my emotion. I was glad that Jeet was there to support me.

Then Auntie Savi hugged me and said, 'I'm sorry for what I've done to you. I realized my mistake after you left us. I've still got your belongings. I kept them thinking that one day you might pop in and collect them. Then I told Sona that I would apologize to you when I saw you again. If I never had the chance, I prayed to God that I would be able to apologize to you in my next life – if there is such a thing. God is great and He answered my prayer in this life.'

'Auntie, I don't believe in killing myself, but the state I was in at that time, I could have done it. I knocked at your door for refuge, but then... Then I thought of my uncles, your brothers. They hadn't done anything to me. I ran away from my problems, but not from them. I prayed to God that I'd live to see this day. As you said, God is great. Because I prayed and prayed hard, God rewarded me with such a wonderful gift – Jeet, two children, and good in-laws. Now my problems are over, I want to help others. Jeet always says we should help wherever we can, and not expect rewards. How could you have done that when I'm your brother's daughter, not a stranger? Yet I'll forgive you.'

Jeet was pleased at the way I had spoken, and said he was proud of me.

After this conversation, I went across and met Sunil's mother and had a long emotional chat with her.

'I'm sorry that I didn't stop to talk to you the other day at the hospital,' I said. 'It was that I felt bitter about the whole thing.'

'I understand,' Sunil's mother replied. 'Don't worry. It's all forgotten.'

'I'm also sorry to hear that Dad is no longer with us.'

'That's all right, daughter,' she replied with a sob. 'He had a heart attack after all the problems with Sunil and the long hours he was doing at work. I kept on telling him to take it easy, but he wouldn't listen.' As she talked, she was continuously drying her tears with her head scarf. I said that I was sorry about her loss.

While I was going round meeting everyone, the women were busy preparing food for us. As soon as

I remembered, I asked, 'By the way Uncle Sona, how is Dada from Camp Maçon?'

'Oh, he died some years ago,' he replied. His wife is still here, but nobody lives there now. You wouldn't recognize the place now.'

'Why not, Uncle?' I asked.

'They've moved to Belle-Vue-Maurel, and they've demolished all the houses at Camp Maçon and planted sugar cane everywhere.'

'I must meet the family sometime. The wife was nice to us.'

Later I said to Uncle Sona, 'Can I have a word with you, Uncle?'

'Yes, what is it?' he replied.

We moved away from others and I asked, 'If you don't mind me asking you, how is your problem with your girlfriend? I know you've suffered a lot, but do you still love her, or see her?'

'Oh, Jaya? Yes, I still love her. You know what they say? "True love never dies". She has some problems, though.'

I knew Jaya, yet I hadn't known Uncle Sona loved her. I also didn't know whether he had mentioned her name deliberately or by mistake.

He continued, 'She couldn't have children and her in-laws thought that she was possessed and sent her back to her parents. She wouldn't tell me whether she aborted herself deliberately because she wasn't happy there, or if it happened naturally. She is at her home and her parents are getting on a bit.'

'Do you want me to talk to her parents, Uncle?'

'No, Chit, they won't listen to you.'

'I can only try. Who knows, Lady Luck may smile on you. I will have to tell Jeet about it, but don't worry, he won't tell anyone.'

'Chit,' Uncle Sona said, 'you're brave.'

'Uncle,' I said, 'I've had to be brave to come this far. So pray God that everything will work out between you and Jaya. I'm sure her parents will be pleased for her sake.'

I talked to Jeet about the problem. He decided to come along with me later. We had dinner at two o'clock and then we went to see Jaya's parents, leaving Ajay and Madhu with their grandmother, who was busy talking to our relatives. Luckily everyone was in at Jaya's house and they were pleased to see me.

I introduced Jeet to them and I started, 'Auntie, it's nice to see you and Jaya as well. Is Jaya spending the weekend with you?'

'No, Chit,' Jaya's mother replied, coming straight to the point, 'she has some problems and, unfortunately, her in-laws sent her back here. It's been a year now, and her husband doesn't want to know her. I heard he was getting married to someone else. We wanted Jaya to marry someone else, but she won't listen to us. We had some people in mind. They came and she made sure that they didn't like her. We're getting old and we don't know what to do. We're afraid that when we die she won't have anyone. She says that she doesn't care.'

'Auntie, Uncle, let me come straight to the point. I think God has answered your prayers.'

At this point Jaya raised her head to see what I was going to say. Auntie said, 'Yes, daughter, we hope that God will listen to our prayers.'

'To cut a long story short,' I continued, 'you know my Uncle Sona? Well he would like to marry Jaya, if you're willing. I don't think Jaya will mind. What do you think of it?'

'Your other uncles should have talked to us, but

142

because we have this problem and we know you, we would like to talk to your Uncle Sona about it. What do you think of it, Jaya?'

There were tears streaming down Jaya's cheeks, and she simply nodded to her mother. Her mother was surprised at this, especially when Jaya had refused to form another relationship previously. Jeet volunteered to go and call Uncle Sona. He was there within 20 minutes.

'Sona,' Jaya's mother said, 'Chit told us that you want to marry Jaya. What's your feeling?'

'I'll marry Jaya if you and Chit agree to this proposal.'

Jaya's eyes were closed. She sat with her head raised and tears rolling down her cheeks. Uncle Sona also couldn't say another word, overcome because he could hardly believe that he could now marry his childhood sweetheart. I felt emotional, but contained myself.

Jaya's mother failed to recognize what was happening, but she said, 'We would have given some time to think over the matter, but because of the problems we're facing, and we're getting on a bit, we have to make an on-the-spot decision. I hope that's a right, and a good decision. I know Jaya's father won't mind. What do you think?'

'I'm all for it if you are,' her father replied.

'We've known Sona a long time and watched him grow up,' Jaya's mother continued. 'He's a nice person, and we accept his decision.'

'Auntie, thank you very much for this lovely meeting. We've got to go now. We'll see you again.'

Jaya's mother continued, 'Chit, we think you're an angel. Now, with that settled, we can die in peace. We'll see you more often now.'

143

'Auntie,' I replied, 'you're an angel for accepting Uncle Sona. You won't regret it.'

Jaya whispered a thank you to me, and Uncle Sona couldn't stop thanking me all the way back home. I told him that if he hadn't mentioned Jaya's name, he would still be grieving.

We managed to catch the bus home at four-thirty. Buses ran on unscheduled timetables, especially on a Sunday, and the last bus went to Port-Louis at six. We had to leave early because Jeet's father wasn't too well. I didn't give my address to anyone but promised to give it to them eventually.

On the way home, Jeet's mother said that she was pleased to see my relatives. Jeet said that he admired the way I spoke to people. He said, 'I keep on wondering where you got this art of talking. I could hardly believe the way you handled your Uncle Sona's problem.'

'Jeet,' I replied, 'as I've told you before, my mother always told me to speak up for myself. She did so herself when she was having problems with Dad. After my parents died, I had to face life on my own and learn to talk so that no obstacle would be insurmountable. So that's the way I learned to talk.'

I have now been married for over 15 years and it seems that I have finally found the love I was searching for. Jeet and I grow fonder of each other as the years go by.

My search for love started when we were living apart from Dad. Because of the way I was treated by him, I was looking for a love that I should have got from my father. Mum died and my search for love was greater than before. I learned to face life although I had experienced some love from Sunil but was let down by him being unfaithful to me.

144

My aunt was rotten to me and this led me into a different sort of life, which I have put down to experience. I continued to search for love, and prayed to God that I would find it.

God was kind, He sent Jeet along. Jeet knew about the life I was living yet he was not deterred by it. Love is great. Jeet is an understanding person and husband, and we are too mature to do anything silly, such as being unfaithful to each other. His parents are nice, and respectful. It now seems to me that the missing piece of my jigsaw puzzle has been found, and it has fitted in beautifully. All my relatives have started coming to our home and now I believe that we're a happy family. Uncle Sona and Jaya are married now – Deep doesn't want him to move out – and despite their age, they've got a beautiful son they've named Prem, which means love.

I still do my part-time nursing job and Jeet has been trying to teach me how to read and write. We've now got a car, so we can go on trips without having to rely on public transport. We're a happy and complete family. The children are growing up and we try our best to give them as much love as we can, but at the same time we're trying not to spoil them. We hope that they'll grow up and continue from where Jeet and I will have left off.